Evermore

The Queen's Alpha Series, Volume 4

W.J. May

Published by Dark Shadow Publishing, 2018.

This is a work of fiction. Similarities to real people, places, or events are entirely coincidental.

EVERMORE

First edition. March 29, 2018.

Copyright © 2018 W.J. May.

Written by W.J. May.

Also by W.J. May

Bit-Lit Series
Lost Vampire
Cost of Blood
Price of Death

Blood Red Series
Courage Runs Red
The Night Watch
Marked by Courage
Forever Night

Daughters of Darkness: Victoria's Journey
Victoria
Huntress
Coveted (A Vampire & Paranormal Romance)
Twisted

Hidden Secrets Saga

Seventh Mark - Part 1
Seventh Mark - Part 2
Marked By Destiny
Compelled
Fate's Intervention
Chosen Three
The Hidden Secrets Saga: The Complete Series

Paranormal Huntress Series
Never Look Back
Coven Master
Alpha's Permission

Prophecy Series
Only the Beginning
White Winter
Secrets of Destiny

The Chronicles of Kerrigan
Rae of Hope
Dark Nebula
House of Cards
Royal Tea
Under Fire
End in Sight
Hidden Darkness
Twisted Together
Mark of Fate

Strength & Power
Last One Standing
Rae of Light
The Chronicles of Kerrigan Box Set Books # 1 - 6

The Chronicles of Kerrigan: Gabriel
Living in the Past
Staring at the Future
Present For Today

The Chronicles of Kerrigan Prequel
Question the Darkness
Into the Darkness
Fight the Darkness
Alone in the Darkness
Lost in Darkness
Christmas Before the Magic
The Chronicles of Kerrigan Prequel Series Books #1-3

The Chronicles of Kerrigan Sequel
A Matter of Time
Time Piece
Second Chance
Glitch in Time
Our Time
Precious Time

THE QUEEN'S ALPHA SERIES

EVERMORE

USA TODAY BESTSELLING AUTHOR

W . J .   M A Y

1

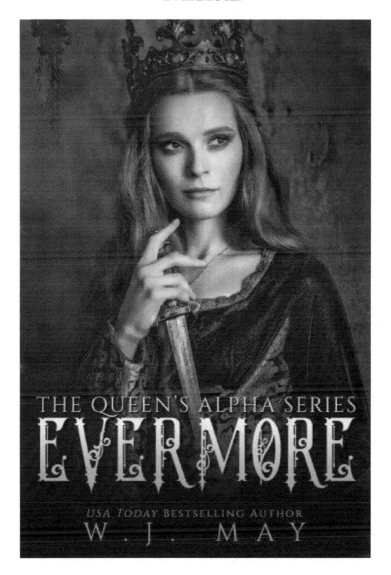

Have You Read the C.o.K Series?

The Chronicles of Kerrigan
Book I - *Rae of Hope* is FREE!

BOOK TRAILER:

http://www.youtube.com/watch?v=gILAwXxx8MU

How hard do you have to shake the family tree to find the truth about the past?

Fifteen year-old Rae Kerrigan never really knew her family's history. Her mother and father died when she was young and it is only when she accepts a scholarship to the prestigious Guilder Boarding School in England that a mysterious family secret is revealed.

Will the sins of the father be the sins of the daughter?

As Rae struggles with new friends, a new school and a star-struck forbidden love, she must also face the ultimate challenge: receive a tattoo on her sixteenth birthday with specific powers that may bind her to an unspeakable darkness. It's up to Rae to undo the dark evil in her family's past and have a ray of hope for her future.

Find W.J. May

Facebook:
https://www.facebook.com/pages/Author-WJ-May-FAN-PAGE/
141170442608149
Newsletter:
SIGN UP FOR W.J. May's Newsletter to find out about new releases, updates, cover reveals and even freebies!
http://eepurl.com/97aYf
Website:
http://www.wanitamay.yolasite.com

EVERMORE Blurb:

She will fight for what is hers.

When Katerina unlocks her secret power and sets the entire royal army ablaze, the stakes to an already- dangerous game soar even higher. As her brother gathers his bannermen to destroy her once and for all, the princess must appeal to the people themselves.

And not just the people. If she wants to take back the throne, she'll need the entire supernatural community by her side.

In a race against time Katerina and her friends scour the country-side, forging new alliances and making new enemies at the same time. Their path is dangerous enough, even without a dark wizard working with her brother. Katerina soon discovers that things aren't always as they seem.

Can the princess rally the support of her people? Can she reconcile the girl she once was with the queen she must become? With all the odds stacked against her...

...can she ever take back the throne?

Be careful who you trust. Even the devil was once an angel.

The Queen's Alpha Series

Eternal
Everlasting
Unceasing
Evermore
Forever

Chapter 1

Katerina had a dream once that she was flying. And not flying the way most people dream it, where they raise their hands and lift off the ground like some kind of human hovercraft. She dreamt that she had been *made* to fly. She was born to it. Instead of lifting her arms, she lifted a pair of giant wings. Wings so immense and powerful that she needed merely to flick the tip of them to move earth and heaven. That with only a whisper of a thought, she would take to the skies.

There wasn't a single other thought in her mind as she soared through the heavens, spanning mountains and miles that would have taken ages to walk on foot. If it weren't for the occasional gasp or sudden tightening of tiny fingers, she wouldn't have even remembered there was a group of stricken people sitting on her back. Instead, she found herself playing a strange vocabulary game.

Euphoric. What's better than euphoric?

A litany of similar words tumbled through her mind, as if she'd swallowed a thesaurus when she was younger like the good little princess she was. Joyous, elated, ecstatic, intoxicated. She came to a sudden pause, thinking the word over with care.

Intoxicated might work. To fly as a dragon was...*intoxicating*. The only time she'd come close to the same blissed-out feeling, the strange out-of-body lightness, was the first time she'd ever found herself drunk at the monastery tavern. Then, of course, there was the feeling she got whenever she found herself lying in Dylan's arms. Whenever their lips pressed together in a stolen kiss.

As if he could feel her thoughts, there was a sudden tightening on the back of Katerina's neck. She glanced over her shoulder and found a set of pale blue eyes staring back at her. Unlike the others, who were clustered together in the middle of her back, gripping hard onto the glinting scales as if they might fall, he looked as though he was born to fly, too. The wind whipped his dark hair away from his eyes, the faint curve of a smile on his lips.

He was as beautiful now, haloed by a radiant display of stars, as he had been the first time she'd ever met him. Cocky. Aloof. Leaning against the sticky counter of the bar as a horde of angry vampires hissed and snarled in his face. She'd been just as taken with him back then. Speechless, in fact. She remembered wondering at what someone like him was doing in such a dismal place. As if he'd been plucked straight from the stars and dropped unceremoniously into a forgotten alley. The difference that set him apart, intangible as it was, positively shone out of him. Putting his attempts to blend in with the others to shame. Lighting him up like a beacon. One she'd found herself drawn to with a pull that no person could withstand. That no person would want to.

Of course, she knew now why that was. Dylan looked like he didn't belong for a very simple reason. He didn't. He couldn't help it any more than he could help the royal blood flowing in his veins. The ancient lineage that no matter of time or distance could ever escape.

In a lot of ways, he was just like her. Shrouding himself in secrets and lies. Putting up invisible walls to keep himself protected from the outside world. Always trying to say a step ahead.

"We should stop soon," he said quietly, knowing she could still hear. "Find a place to set up camp for the night. The rest of us need rest. And food—" He hesitated, and the words he stopped himself from saying rang suddenly between them.

Not sure if YOU need those things...

A deep-throated rumble of laughter echoed in the hollows of the princess' chest, and she glanced back again with a dragon's teasing approximation of a smile.

Is someone getting a little nervous? her arched eyebrows seemed to say. *Afraid we might keep circling around up here forever? Or worried that I might be getting a little hungry myself?*

He stared at her a moment in open wonder, still baffled by the transformation that had happened before his very eyes, before he pulled back. A little grin was dancing around his face as he angled defensively behind one of the rigid spines upon her back.

"I wasn't volunteering..."

She laughed again but lowered her head down through the clouds as she began searching the countryside for a place to land. It was hard to tell exactly how long they'd been flying. The concept of time was distinctly foreign to a dragon. Along with things like subtlety and scale. All she knew was that when they'd left Talsing, the sun had been setting. Now, it had long since gone down. The blazing sunset had been replaced with a bank of stars. Like the shimmering sands of a seashore. So close, she felt as though she could almost touch them.

There was a gentle nudge on the base of her neck and she nodded. Both she and Dylan had spotted it at the same time. A little clearing tucked away inside a thick cluster of trees. Isolated enough to provide adequate protection, and open enough to allow space for a dragon to land.

With a sudden burst of speed she arched her wings and shot toward the ground like a flaming arrow, silently reveling in the petrified screams that echoed in her wake. Of course, one person wasn't screaming. There was a short burst of delighted laughter, but it was quickly silenced with a punishing *thwack*. Her lips curled into an unmistakable grin. She could almost picture Cassiel hitting Dylan upside the back of the head, the look of fury on his angelic face.

A current of wind billowed her wings like the sail of a ship, and the next thing she knew they were gliding. Soaring low along the top of the forest, so close that one needed only to reach over to touch the tips of the trees.

It isn't so hard, is it? Flying. Easiest thing in the world.

Katerina circled around once, spotted the open field of grass, then angled her body effortlessly towards it—coming down with out-stretched talons.

Landing? Landing proved to be another story...

"SEVEN HELLS!"

There was a discordant chorus of shrieks and profanities behind her, and the princess flinched apologetically as she dug her serrated claws into the earth—leaving deep gouges behind as she tried desperately to slow their speed. In the end, there was nothing to be done. Her passengers collectively 'jumped ship' a second before she braced her body and smashed into the trees.

At this point, she wouldn't mind a few broken bones if it meant slowing her impossible momentum. But, as it turned out, she didn't need to worry about her body so much as the unfortunate piece of forest she used to break her fall.

There was a high-pitched wail, the sound of screeching wood, as the ancient redwoods split open beneath her. Splintering as easily as toothpicks as she slid to a slow stop. The smell of sap hung sharp in the air, mixing with the aroma of freshly shredded leaves. It was embarrassing enough on its own, but when she looked up a second later she saw four anxious faces peering back at her.

This is going to become one of those things, isn't it? Those jokes you can't get away from. She pulled herself stiffly to her feet, trying to maintain as much dignity as possible as she preemptively braced for what was sure to come. *'Remember that time you accidentally took out a centuries-old forest because you couldn't figure out how to land?' 'The woodland creatures called; they want their home back...'*

A round of slow applause started up from the edge of the clearing, and she knew it was going to be just as bad as she thought. However, one person wasn't clapping. Cassiel, who still hadn't forgiven her for shifting in the first place, looked like he was about to be sick. Dylan clapped him on the shoulder with a wide grin as he trudged through the trampled underbrush to meet her.

"Quite the show, Your Highness." His eyes twinkled as they looked her up and down. It didn't seem to matter that she was currently a dragon. Fevered chills swept over her body with just a brush of his gaze. "Ready to join the rest of us mere mortals?"

She took a step towards him, then froze suddenly in place. A wave of panic flooded through her, paralyzing every inch as she suddenly realized there was something harder than landing.

Shifting back.

"It's all right." True to form, Dylan read her panic as clearly as if it was his own. Completely ignoring the others behind him he closed the distance between them, lowering his voice and placing a reassuring hand on her side. "It's always hard the first time—you just need to calm down. Take a deep breath. Try to relax."

She exhaled loudly, trying to do as he asked. A cloud of fire shot from her mouth and lit a nearby tree on fire. Missing his head by just inches.

He ducked automatically then straightened up, looking a little pale.

"Okay, maybe not so much with the deep breaths." She hung her head miserably but he stroked a hand along the side of her neck, laughing softly. "Let's just try again, shall we? Close your eyes, Katerina. Listen to the sound of my voice."

She wondered if he'd said her name on purpose. She didn't feel much like Katerina Damaris in this new body. She felt like something much, much more. But at the sound of her name, she was suddenly reminded of the girl she was. The girl, not the dragon. Red hair, grey eyes.

A tendency to trip over things and fall that some might label as clumsy. She found it rather endearing herself.

There was a gasp from somewhere in the distance, and the princess found herself suddenly cold. A soft rush of air whistled through her ears, and before she could even open her eyes she was standing on the forest floor. A cold sheet of pine needles clung to the bottoms of her bare feet, and she shivered as the forest mist prickled her arms. Her hair swished gently down the center of her back, tickling the skin in a way that was as comforting and familiar, as it was suddenly terrifying.

Her *bare* feet? The *skin* on her back?

Katerina's eyes snapped open in horror.

Sure enough... she was naked.

A thousand silent screams echoed through her head as she woke up from what felt like a magical dream into a real-life nightmare. Standing naked in the middle of the woods. Her friends' eyes upon her. Her dress and travelling cloak left back at the monastery. Assumedly strewn along the jagged rocks that lined the bottom of the cliff.

Hot, visceral panic shot through her and she just was contemplating the sudden urge to run, when a soft voice broke through her horrified trance.

"There, that's better."

She lifted her head to see Dylan staring at her from just a few feet away, a look of tender affection spilling softly across his face.

Dylan, the king of sarcasm himself. The man who forbid himself to take anything seriously and aggravated every possible situation with a searing joke... had nothing to say.

She shivered again as he took a step towards her, but he was calm and serene. His eyes never dipped below her chin. Not a hint of that telltale mischief was left on his face.

Without a word he slipped off his cloak and draped it over her shoulders, taking care to avoid touching her bare skin while he simultaneously shielded her from view. Her fingers hastened to tie the leather straps, scrabbling clumsily with nerves and cold, but when she finally dared to look at him once more he was offering his arm with a gentle smile.

"Shall we?"

Something about seeing him breathe made it easier for her to breathe as well. After a frozen moment of indecision, her lungs started working again and she laced her arm through his.

"Yeah... thanks."

He nodded, as though he talked naked girls through dragon transformations every day, and the two of them started walking back to the others in the clearing. It wasn't until they were halfway there that his lips twitched up with the hint of a grin.

"...freak."

"THAT WAS ABSOLUTELY unacceptable!"

The fire was roaring, the meat was roasting, and for the most part the little company of friends was in fine spirits. The only exception was the fae, who hovered on the periphery of the circle with a vicious glare. One that intensified every time it came to rest on Katerina.

"Oh, would you give it a rest, already?" Tanya threw a piece of venison at him, rolling her eyes as she settled back to watch the flames. "We've all gotten past it."

"Speak for yourself," Rose inserted, leaning forward to tear another helping off the hunk of meat skewered through the center of the pyre. "I think that flight shaved twenty years off my life."

Katerina bit her lip, but Dylan laced his arm around her waist—pulling her against his side with a beaming smile. Instead of fretting she felt herself flush with pride, nestling into the warmth of his jacket with a little grin.

"Better twenty years than sixty," he said matter-of-factly. "If Kat hadn't done what she did, precisely when she did it, we'd all be back at the monastery. Pretty little piles of ash."

A collective shudder ran through the group as everyone abruptly grew quiet. Even Cassiel abandoned his anger long enough to look momentarily thoughtful before glancing up once more.

"...but a *dragon*?"

"What's so wrong with dragons?" Katerina laughed, throwing up her hands. It was much easier to talk about it with a full belly and Dylan's arm wrapped snugly around her side. "Would you have preferred I turned into a hummingbird? Might have had a hard time carrying you then..."

Considering Cassiel was one of the most unshakably pragmatic people she knew, he discarded this obvious logic with a wave of his hand. "Dragons are frightful beasts. Worse than anything else in the five kingdoms. I should have known a *Damaris* would shift into one of them."

A few weeks ago, Katerina would have been stung to the core. Now, she leaned forward with a teasing grin. Like a mischievous child who delighted in poking a bear.

"I'm so sorry, Cass. I didn't know that *me saving your life* would have such a devastating effect on your delicate sensibilities. Here," she half-pushed to her feet, "why don't I just fly you back—"

She didn't know what knocked her down. Dylan's arm, pulling her back to his side, or the hunk of meat Cassiel lobbed right into her sternum. Either way, she sank back with a smirk, pleased to see that the fae was grinning as well. He was still shaken, undeniably shaken, but grinning.

"Sleep well tonight, princess. Rest assured I won't smother you in your sleep..."

Tanya ignored all of them as if they hadn't even been talking. After Dylan, she had been the quickest one to come to terms with Katerina's new ability, and after just a few hours of marveling, the dazzling magic transformation had already rolled off her impervious little back.

"Can we *please* circle back to the issue at hand?" When Tanya asked things like that, it was rarely ever a question. "The army is gone, but so is the safe house. We're out here in the middle of nowhere, and it's only a matter of time before news of this spreads."

Rose tilted her head to the side, eyes sparkling dual colors by the light of the flames. "None of that was actually a question—"

"What are we going to *do*?"

For the first time since the disastrous landing and the dinner that followed, the friends grew quiet. It was easy to make jokes and distractions when the smoldering wreckage of what you'd left behind was just that—*behind* you. But what about the trials still to come? They'd come so far, been through so much, but in a lot of ways they were back exactly where they'd started.

"To start, the army isn't *gone*," Dylan said slowly. "A battalion of it, maybe, but the rest is still back with your brother at the castle." His eyes flickered to Katerina. "And I imagine it's only a matter of time before he decides to replenish his ranks."

She gazed at him curiously, a little embarrassed that he knew more about the military ins and outs of castle politics than she did. *Then again, he would, wouldn't he?* Her eyes widened with curiosity as she suddenly wondered if he'd ever had a battalion to command himself. Back at his own castle.

"What does that mean?" she asked quietly. "Replenish the ranks."

"He's going to call in his bannermen." It was Cassiel who replied, and he did so with the grim assurance of one who'd seen it happen before. "Great houses and cities throughout the kingdom who've pledged their allegiance to the crown. They'll all be called upon to fight."

"Then, why let him?" Rose asked suddenly. Her presence was still a bit unusual, especially considering the well-established dynamic of the group. Yet, somehow, it was already easy to think of her as part of the gang. "You guys saw what Katerina did back there. She took out an entire *battalion* of the royal army in, like, six seconds! Why not fly to the castle and do it again?"

It was a fair question. Again, the gang fell silent. Lost in thought.

Why NOT just fly back to the castle? Why NOT douse the rest of the army in flames?

It wasn't like they would ever stop coming after her. With the throne itself at stake, Kailas wouldn't rest until she was dead. They would just keep coming. Battalion after battalion. It wasn't like those battalions didn't leave a trail of innocent casualties in their wake, and after over two months of hiding out in the wilderness, awash with fear, it was hard to argue against any plan that could effectively end the war in a matter of minutes.

But end it how?

Katerina's face tightened as she stared into the flames. Much as she tried to forget, she could remember every stricken face that had tilted upwards as she soared overhead. She remembered every tortured scream. The look of blind terror shining in their eyes.

Ducks in a barrel.

She remembered her brother's cruel words. Right before he and his hunting party massacred the trapped herd of snow-white deer. Their screams didn't sound so different from the ones she'd heard before. From the scores of men fleeing for their lives. Fleeing in a fight not their own.

Death was death. No matter the cost. No matter the scale.

It should never be dealt with a heavy hand.

"No."

Her voice was quiet but decided. Sitting around the fire her friends lifted their heads to look at her, one by one.

"The throne is mine," she continued firmly, "and I intend to take it back. But you can't rule a kingdom of corpses. Whatever judgement passes on my brother, it's for him and him alone. I won't let the people suffer for his misdeeds. No matter what that means for me."

Dylan turned to face her, his eyes blazing with pride.

"Then, where does that leave us?" Tanya asked again. The girl was a survivor first, and a martyr second. But over the last few weeks, Katerina had seen a shockingly selfless side emerge.

"It leaves us in the middle of a war." Cassiel's face was harder to read, but if Katerina wasn't mistaken she'd swear there was a hint of pride there as well. "Whether you fight them as a dragon or not—the army *will* fight. If you don't want to annihilate them outright, you'll need people of your own. People willing to *take up the cause.*"

He stressed the last words in a way Katerina didn't understand and turned to look squarely at Dylan. Dylan closed his eyes with a wince and muttered, "I was *really* hoping to avoid that..."

"What?"

It was Tanya who had asked the question, but all three girls were staring at the guys with matching looks of curiosity. Cassiel's eyes lit up with the ghost of a smile.

"Ask Dylan how he and I met."

Dylan's eyes shot open and he shot his friend a pained look, deliberately avoiding Katerina's eyes all the while. The princess, however, wasn't so easy to avoid. Especially sitting two inches away.

"What is he talking about?" She poked him sharply in the ribs. "Dylan?"

He winced again. More at the question than at the poking.

"It's one of those things that sounds worse when you say it out loud."

She slid out from under his arm, twisting around with a demanding stare.

"*Tell me.*"

The time for secrets between them had passed. Burned up in the fires at the monastery. It was the time now for hard truths. No matter how potentially painful they might be.

She knew it. Dylan knew it, too.

He raked his fingers through his hair, a nervous gesture that doubled as a stalling tactic when necessary. "Keeping in perspective, this was before I knew you. And it was *certainly* before I knew you could turn into a dragon who could eat us all—"

"*Dylan.*"

He winced again and Cassiel leaned forward with a smile, more than happy to take over the story himself. "I met Dylan up north—organizing one of the rebel camps."

Katerina blanked. The words were all familiar, and yet...

"The rebel camps?"

The fae grinned. Somehow managing to look both beautiful and terrifying at the same time.

"The point of which were to wipe you and your family off the face of the map."

Rose and Tanya looked deliberately down at their hands, while Katerina turned to Dylan in open-mouthed astonishment. "Is that true?"

His eyes flashed up with an apologetic grimace. Wavy hair spilling into his face.

"That was the tentative agenda... yeah."

Chapter 2

When Katerina opened her eyes the next morning the embers were still burning low in the fire, crackling and hissing as they turned gradually into ash. She watched them for a moment, letting herself adjust to the pale grey light, then her gaze drifted slowly over the rest of the campsite.

For a split second, she almost smiled.

Her beloved new friends might have been as tough and jaded as they came, but at the moment they looked like the victims of a slumber party gone wrong. Hair was tangled into hair—different colors knotted together. Limbs were splayed across limbs. In lieu of a tent or any kind of blanket, they had once again huddled together for warmth beside the fire. It was nothing they hadn't done before, but the addition of Rose added a new dynamic. One that made things feel a little more crowded than they had before.

The smile crept up the side of Katerina's face as she stared down with fond affection. She wondered what the fae prince would say if he could see himself now. Wedged unceremoniously in between the bodies of two shifters. She wondered what Tanya would say when she found out her boyfriend had accidentally wound his arm around the wrong set of shoulders in his sleep.

That's one argument I'll gladly miss.

With a little pivot that was becoming almost habitual she turned on her heel and headed off through the trees, towards the outer rim of the forest where the great redwoods gave way to a magnificent view of the valley beyond. Streaked with patches of early sunlight and veined with so many rivers and creeks, she wondered if they could paddle successfully from one side to the other.

It was a gorgeous view, to be sure, but not so beautiful as the man looking over it. He stood with his back to her, shoulders slightly tensed against the cold as his eyes roved out over the patchwork of blues and greens. But she could tell he heard her coming, because he tilted his head to the side with the slightest of grins.

"I thought princesses were supposed to sleep in. Pass out in a pile of cushions, wake up at noon, throwing crystal stemware and demanding pastries. Kind of like demented cats."

Katerina snorted and came up behind him, wrapping her thin arms around his sides as she buried her chilly fingers in the pockets of his jacket. "You would know. You meet a lot of spoiled princesses back in your day? Throw a lot of crystal stemware?"

His body tensed, but he didn't answer. To be honest, he seemed more surprised by her casual embrace than he was by the question. Their talk back at the monastery was supposed to have sorted things out—cut the cord and made it clear why the two of them could never be together. But as far as the princess was concerned, things had never been more tangled.

I love you. You love me. So, tell me again... what's the problem?

"That's..." He glanced down, the tips of his dark hair spilling into his eyes as he stared at their joint connection. "No, I didn't."

His voice was unexpectedly quiet, and for the first time Katerina stiffened as if she might have done something wrong. She moved to retract her hands, but before she could he turned around in a fluid, graceful movement. His arms circled around her back, and the next thing she knew he was holding her tight against his chest. Eyes twinkling with a little smile.

"I like to be on top."

She stared up at him, breathless and flushed pink with surprise. "What?"

He cocked a devilish eyebrow and glanced pointedly at their arms. His embrace was warm and comforting, but it left him completely in control. Her own arms were pinned to her sides. "The guy holding the reins, the big spoon... need I continue?"

His arms squeezed a little tighter, adding a dose of levity to the situation, and Katerina let out her breath with a nervous laugh. "And what if I want to be the big spoon?"

She tried teasingly to move her arms, but he didn't budge an inch. If she didn't know better, she'd swear he hadn't even noticed she was trying.

"Well, you'd have to fight me for it." He leaned down so their faces were just inches apart, his eyes teeming with mischief. "And I can't say I like your chances..."

Normally, Katerina would have backed down. She would have retreated clumsily from the conversation, cheeks blazing, and proceeded to overanalyze every word for the remainder of the day. But things weren't really 'normal' anymore. And neither was Katerina.

"My chances?" Even though they were already toe to toe she took a step closer, forcing him to stumble back. "Aww, *puppy*... have you forgotten which one of us can breathe fire?"

A look of true astonishment flitted across his face. Whether it was from having his own dazzling transformation into a lupine predator reduced to a mere 'puppy' or from her casual reference to her own supernatural gifts, Katerina didn't know.

But it was a clear win. Of that she was sure.

Ding—round one!

There was a split second of silence, then he released her with a soft, "Touché."

They stepped apart, still smiling, but his faded as another emotion came slowly to light. One that was casual but pressing. Like a leaf floating up to the rippling face of a pond. By the time it reached the surface, it had tightened into wordless concern.

"What is it?" she asked automatically, fighting the urge to take his hand. What was it about strong men that made you want to protect them so badly? An overdeveloped sense of irony?

He hesitated, so long that Katerina didn't think he was going to answer, then he raised those piercing eyes of his to her face. "Did you know what was going to happen? When you jumped over the side of the cliff?"

It was a testament to how quickly their world was shifting that she hadn't given much thought to the question until now. She remembered the way her toes had scrunched together as they left the stone ledge behind her and stepped into nothing but air. She remembered the look on his face not a moment before, how he would have given anything he had for her not to.

"Not exactly," she confessed. Borrowing a move of his she ran a distracted hand through her hair, fingers tangling in the unkempt snarls. "I didn't know what would happen, but I knew that it was what I was supposed to do—if that makes any sense. It was a weird feeling, but a calming one at the same time. I trusted it."

It was quiet for a long time before she looked up sharply. Her eyes swept once over his handsome face before turning the same question right around on him.

"What about you?" she asked softly, tilting her head to catch his eye. "Did you know what would happen when *you* jumped?"

He glanced up in surprise. It seemed like she couldn't stop surprising him that morning.

"I thought I did." He laughed darkly, then his face cleared with an honest smile. "But I hadn't counted on Michael."

Katerina gave him a curious frown, but just as suddenly she understood.

Michael.

An image of an enormous, majestic eagle flashed through her mind—pulling wounded men off the battlefield and flying them back to safety. She could only imagine the scene that must have taken place just four years ago. When a younger version of Dylan leapt off the wall, only to find himself immediately overtaken by the wings of the massive bird.

She chuckled quietly, unable to stop herself. "That must have been a bit of a shock."

He laughed freely, able to see it with a better perspective after all this time. "A *shock*. That's one way of putting it. I fought him off as best I could, you know. I had no idea the thing was Michael, and my idea of a perfect death wasn't ending up in the belly of a bird."

Katerina laughed again, then quieted just as suddenly. A sharp pang echoed through her heart as she lifted her eyes to his. "And that's really what you wanted?" It came out barely louder than a whisper. "You wanted to die?"

The smile melted off his face, and he bowed his head. Despite the few months that separated them, he suddenly looked years older. Burdened with sorrows beyond his time. "No," he finally answered, "I didn't want to die."

"But, then—"

"I didn't see any other way out." His face tightened with a distant sort of pain, one that the passage of time couldn't seem to erase. "To know the terrible things my family had done, the people they'd killed... the *weight* of that. I felt like it was killing me. But then, when my own parents were killed, my aunts and cousins and uncles, I still felt..."

He trailed off, looking a little lost, and Katerina slipped her hand into his.

"Grief?"

His fingers flinched at the word, like it was some kind of accusation, but he nodded his head with a sigh. "I know I shouldn't have. They deserved their punishment. Each one. I know that it was wrong to mourn their loss, but I couldn't help it. They were my family. Everything I knew."

The princess' heart broke, and without thinking she slid her hands up his arms all the way to his face, cupping it gently as she stared up into his eyes. "It was not *wrong* for you to grieve the loss of your family. To grieve is human. No matter what they did, they were your flesh and blood."

"Exactly. My own flesh and blood." His eyes cooled for a moment with indescribable anger before softening just as suddenly with unbearable pain. "So much blood." The word lifted out of him, like it had wings itself. "That's exactly what I was thinking up on that ledge. That my entire life was colored with other people's blood. The day that I jumped... I guess I just wanted it all to stop."

Katerina slowly lowered her hands to her sides, staring silently at the man in front of her. A man who had seen more bloodshed and pain in his eighteen short years than most people would see in a lifetime. A man who'd been forced to grow up too fast, leaving the wide-eyed boy behind.

"So, what changed?" she asked quietly.

It was like lifting a veil. The shadows that had fallen over him brightened until there were none left, vanishing entirely as he lifted his eyes to the brilliant sunrise.

"Michael."

A single word to answer a complicated question, but it was enough. Katerina got the sense that that single word had been the answer to many questions he'd asked himself over the years.

"After chaining me to a chair in his office, making me swear I wouldn't try to hurt myself again, he taught me an important lesson: You can't change the past; you can only change the future."

A touch of amusement flashed across his face, and he shot Katerina a little grin.

"He tried to teach me a lot more than that, but I wasn't the most receptive student."

She laughed, having no trouble believing that. Dylan could be introspective and thoughtful when he wanted to be, but she couldn't picture him consigned to a classroom.

"But that one lesson, those words, stuck." All at once, he was serious again. His face distant as he thought back to times gone by. "I trained hard. Learned my craft. Dedicated myself day and night to pushing every limit. To finding out exactly what I was able to do. Two years later to the day, I set out for the northern territories. Determined to make a change."

There was so much to say. So many gaps to fill in. But Katerina let them all pass. She hadn't been with him back then. The important thing was that she was with him now.

"At which point you met up with the rebel camps and decided to assassinate yours truly."

His eyes flashed up quickly, as if he'd been lost in a dream, before crinkling with an adorable sort of apology. "...yes?"

She couldn't help but laugh. When the man you've fallen in love with admits to having once dedicated his life to your demise, laughter is the only—if ironic—response. "Well, let's just hope that everyone still over there doesn't share your sentiments." She made the conscious effort to stifle a shudder. "At least, not about me."

Two hands came up immediately, gripping her shoulders.

"Kat, that isn't something you need to worry about. Them harming you. I would never let us go otherwise." His eyes locked onto hers, holding them firm. "You have my word."

She stared at him for a moment, then nodded quickly. The truth was, she wasn't all that anxious about what resistance she, personally, might find in the rebel camps. She was more worried about the step that came next. The one that involved her twin brother.

It was not wrong for you to grieve the loss of your family. To grieve is human. No matter what they did, they were your flesh and blood.

Her own words echoed back to her, sounding suddenly cheap and hollow. The might be true. Hell, they were certainly relevant. But they were hardly a comfort. She wondered if Dylan had felt the same.

"Come on," he held out his hand, cocking his head back towards the trees, "we're going to want to get an early start if we're to make it to the camps by nightfall."

Katerina accepted the hand without thinking, wrapping her fingers through his own with a teasing grumble. "Or we could let everyone sleep in, then I could just fly us over sometime in the evening after a leisurely meal. There's hardly a need to walk on foot anymore, you know."

Dylan chuckled, marching purposely across the grass. "Well, much as I *love* the naked landing, I'm not sure the fae's nerves could handle another ride. Not to mention the fact that we'd like to keep your little secret from reaching the castle for as long as possible. The more times you do it out in the open, the better the chances your brother will find out."

Katerina nodded along, but she'd heard little after the words 'naked landing.' As it stood, she wasn't wearing a stitch of clothing under his cloak, and the slightest gust of breeze was enough to send her into a mild panic attack. What was worse, she had a sudden suspicion that Dylan knew this, given the sly shifting of his eyes every time the wind angled their way.

"Well, I'm glad you enjoyed it," she said acidly, ignoring the rest of what he said and focusing only on that mortifying phrase. "But the show's over. It was a one-time occurrence."

His teeth sank into his lower lip to prevent a smile as one hand lifted to his chest with a look of mock-heartbreak. "That has to be the saddest thing I've ever heard."

"Oh, shut up."

"I must find a way to convince you otherwise."

"Shut up, or I'll light you on fire."

"What if I took off my clothes first? Would that make things any better?"

Acting on impulse she pulled him to a sudden stop, wrapping her fingers around his sleeve as her eyes darted reflexively in the general direction of their friends. He pulled up short with a look of surprise, gazing down with a question twinkling in his eyes.

"I didn't mean right *now*, but if you insist—"

"The things you said," she interrupted, "back at the monastery. How we could never be together, and things would unravel when we got to the castle. I didn't... what I mean is, I'm not—"

He silenced her with a kiss. A deep kiss. The kind that took her breath away.

One second, they were talking, and the next she was standing on the tips of her toes. His hands were winding through her hair, his lips were expertly parting hers, and as the wind picked up her cloak flew open to expose her bare legs up to the thigh.

She pulled away with a gasp to pull the fabric shut as he glanced down with a roguish grin.

"And here I thought the show was over—"

"What the heck was that?" she interrupted. Her head was spinning, her fingers and toes were tingling, and there was a slight ringing in her ears. "I thought you said—"

"Princess," his eyes twinkled, and he gave her a little wink, "we're not at the castle yet."

...*oh.*

Katerina truly had no idea what to say to this. She wouldn't have trusted herself to speak, even if she had been able to come up with something clever. Instead, she merely walked along beside him back towards the camp, studiously avoiding his eyes as her cheeks flushed scarlet.

It wasn't until they were nearly there that he glanced down with a parting shot.

"Oh, and Katerina, don't ever call me *puppy*."

The silence came to an abrupt stop. Taking that shy, blushing girl with it.

"I think I will." A wide grin stretched from ear to ear as she patted him lightly on the head and flounced away. "I think it's the beginning of a whole new chapter."

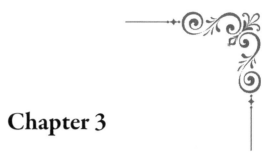

Chapter 3

By the time Dylan and Katerina got back to camp, the rest of the gang was already awake and moving. The remains of yesterday's deer was crackling on the fire. The inevitable fight from their unfortunate sleeping arrangements had apparently passed leaving Tanya scowling, Rose looking smug, and Cassiel uncharacteristically meek. When the couple walked into the clearing, still discreetly holding hands, they were greeted with a trio of smiles.

"Venison?" Rose tossed Katerina a chunk of dripping meat, flashing a broad grin as the princess automatically wrinkled up her nose. "It's even better the day after."

While the others had grown to regard Katerina's royal heritage as nothing more than an eccentric and inconvenient personality quirk, Rose seemed to find the entire thing greatly amusing. The sight of the princess in training clothes, sweating it out on the bridge line, or even forcing down what Grinelda—the old hag who worked in the monastery kitchen—had sarcastically referred to as 'porridge' had become one of her favorite pastimes. Today was proving to be no exception.

Katerina passed the meat to Dylan, who scarfed it down in maybe three bites. "I'll take your word for it." She bypassed the bonfire entirely and went for the fruit instead. "Thanks, though."

The shifter's grin stretched even wider. "Oh, that's right, I shouldn't have cooked it. I keep forgetting that you probably like it better raw."

It took Katerina a full five seconds to realize she was making a joke about dragons. Another five seconds after that to remember that jokes about dragons now applied to her. Fortunately, it took no time at all to fire back a barb of her own.

"Sleep well?" she asked sweetly, resurrecting a recently buried hatchet. "All warm and cozy?"

Rose's grin faded, and she shot Tanya a nervous glance. The shifter was sharpening her blade against the side of a flattened rock, sending periodic showers of sparks from the razor-edge. When she felt the wolf girl's eyes upon her, she lifted her head with a smile just as sweet.

"So, what's the plan for today?" Cassiel asked quickly. He was usually the one helping to formulate the plan himself, but in this case his only desire was to swiftly move the conversation forward. His eyes fell on Dylan with a silent cry for help. "Are we taking Bowline Trail or cutting straight through by the river?"

Katerina's eyes flashed once more towards the valley, though it was now hidden behind a curtain of trees. The entire grassy basin seemed to be a winding tangle of rivers. At this point, she didn't really see how they could avoid them. As usual, Dylan seemed to be thinking the same thing.

"We'll cut through," he said decisively, stepping casually in between Cassiel and the shifters at the same time. "Stick to the shoreline. With any luck, we can make it across by tomorrow."

"With any luck?" Tanya snorted and pushed stiffly to her feet. Apparently, the midnight flight wasn't proving so fun the day after. "Since when did we have any of that?"

"Hey, that's not true." Rose offered her a tentative, conciliatory smile. "We didn't burn to death in the monastery, did we? Didn't even get shot! Maybe I'm your good luck charm."

Tanya cast her a pained look, and Dylan shook his head with a grimace. "Our standards have gotten impossibly strange."

Rose coughed, trying to cover up a laugh. "And Katerina didn't even eat us for dinner!"

CONSIDERING SOME OF the places Katerina had been in the last two months, the northern river basin turned out to be exceptionally beautiful. The tall grass folded gently underfoot, whispering in the breeze as they walked beside the sparkling water. Around every twist and turn grew yet another cluster of shaded fruit trees offering everything from apples to pears to plums. Multi-colored birds called back and forth to each other, lightening the air with sweet voices lilting in song as their vibrant wings fluttered up and down with the beat.

And the best part of all? For the first time in months, they weren't being followed.

"Stick close together. No one falls behind."

Of course, not everyone was having such an easy time letting down their guard.

With scarcely-contained sighs of exasperation the others adjusted their pace and clustered closer around the ranger, sealing Katerina automatically in the middle of their circle as they marched through the sparkling fairy world in lock-step.

It continued like this all through the day. Starting in the morning, growing worse through the afternoon, and continuing on as the sun arced slowly across the sky.

The easier the road got, the warier Dylan seemed to become. The more fragrant the wildflowers that scented the air, the tighter the clench of his jaw. When a fawn pranced suddenly across the path, Katerina was worried he was going to wolf-out right then and there.

"Tanya, put that flask away. I need you sharp."

By now the sun was beginning to set, and the whiskey turned out to be the last straw. Tanya reached for her dagger with a rather stoic expression, and after many pleading looks from the others the princess attempted to intervene.

"Honey, you've got to loosen up." Katerina slipped her arm through Dylan's, struggling a bit to do so because he kept one hand anchored to the handle of his blade. "You said it yourself, there's no one around for miles. Nobody's on our trail. Try to relax a little."

The others cast hopeful glances, but Cassiel shook his head with a grin. Only he seemed to sense what was going to happen next. Sure enough, Dylan didn't disappoint.

"Relax?" There was no inflection in his voice, and he kept his eyes fixed on the breathtaking horizon. "You let your guard down, people slip past. You loosen up, that's when everything starts to go sideways." He shook his head, stiff as a soldier. "You relax, you die."

Well, that's a cheery outlook.

The princess lapsed into silence as the others gave up the ghost. They might have been walking through a delightful little wonderland, but apparently none of that wonder was for them. It wasn't until a few minutes had passed that Dylan turned back to her suddenly.

"Did you just call me '*honey*'?"

Katerina's face flushed as she realized her mistake. Then, just as quickly, she decided to stand by it. *At least it wasn't 'puppy'. He's called me pet names before. What? He's the only one who gets to use them?* She deflected the crux of the question with a joke. "I'm sorry. Is this not the right place for something like that? With danger about to jump out from every corner?" He shot her a hard look, and her smile faded. "Why don't we call it a day?" she asked softly, contemplating the chances of group mutiny if he were to refuse. "The sun's starting to go down, we could set up camp and—"

"I don't want to stop here," he said shortly. "We can go for a few more hours."

A few more hours?!

The girls shot each other looks of despair while Cassiel abandoned his position in the lead with a quiet chuckle, doubling back to fall in step beside his friend.

Whatever unspoken bonds the rest of them were creating, he and Dylan went back a long way. In times of true panic or terror, they turned to each other. Trusting implicitly. Teasing mercilessly. Sharing a silent sort of telepathy that made Katerina as jealous as she was amused.

"You remember the explosion at that gravel mill?" Cass asked casually, matching his friend's long stride. "When the miller's cat ran on to the post and knocked the torch down into the tunnels?"

Dylan glanced at him in surprise, then smiled in spite of himself. "The one where everyone ran back to the fort, but you insisted we stay behind and rescue the cat?"

"That's the one."

"Of course, I remember, you lunatic. That was the first time it became clear to me that you'd be the eventual cause of my death. But what does that have to do with—"

"What about when we were pinned down by Tugali warriors?" Cassiel's eyes danced with the light reflecting off the water. "I thought for sure they had us beat, but you kicked down the door to the laundry shoot and we tumbled out somewhere downstream."

Their pace slowed slightly as Dylan laughed, taking his hand off the handle of his blade to rake it back through his hair. He didn't seem to realize it himself. "We spent the rest of the night in a dug-out canoe," he recalled with a grin. "Singing sea shanties and drinking whatever was left of the lieutenant's wine." He brightened with the fleeting memory, then shot his friend a curious look. "Why are you—"

"Then there was that time in the djinn's tomb, when you got bit by that venomous spider and started hallucinating that you were going to die."

"Cass—"

"I dragged you back to the village, but by the time we got there the place was overrun with Kasi mercenaries and I had to hide you in a pile of leaves."

Dylan held up a hand, his face tightening with a frown. "And as much as I *love* reliving every grisly brush with death, why the heck are you—"

"I'm getting those same vibes right now." The fae's eyes narrowed suspiciously as they swept over the blossoms on the trees. They narrowed some more at the rainbows of light misting up by the nearby falls. A chill ran through his body, and he folded his arms firmly over his chest. Looking, for all intents and purposes, very much the same way that Dylan had been looking for the bulk of the day. "*Bad* vibes. Like, at any moment, the world might come crashing down..."

The girls giggled as Dylan shot him a sour look.

"Okay, I get what you're saying, but I'm not—"

Cassiel's arm flew out to stop him as a tiny rabbit hopped suddenly into their path, the leaves of a sunflower crumpled in its mouth. For a moment, it was comically still. The two sides simply stared at each other. Man versus beast. Then Cassiel lifted a finger, pointing as if the thing had fangs.

"What do you say?" he murmured under his breath. "Shall we fight hand-to-hand, or just unleash the dragon?"

There was a pause. Then Dylan bowed his head. "Maybe I'm being a bit paranoid?"

Cassiel pursed his lips. "Just a little."

The ranger's shoulders wilted as the rabbit vanished in a blur of fur and pollen. To make matters worse, it left a little trail of yellow petals scattered in its wake. Dylan's eyes fell upon them, painfully aware of the irony, before he gestured around with a defeated sigh. "I guess there are worse places to set up camp."

An actual cheer rose up from the rest of them as they set down their paltry belongings and settled down into the tall grass. None was more relieved than Katerina. While her travelling companions might have been used to ten-hour walks and sleeping under the stars, she was still relatively new to the game. And while she swore to herself she'd never complain, that didn't stop her from taking great comfort when the long days finally came to an end.

In this land, they didn't need to be too specific in terms of finding adequate shelter. The air was warm, the clouds were miles away, and one place was as good as another. They cast off their weapons with a sigh, leaning against the smooth trunks of the trees. Gazing out over the river as the fading sunlight glittered and danced across the top of the waves. Stretching out their stiff bodies, over-hardened from travel, but finally contented with the promise of sleep.

"Whiskey, anyone?" The flask was out, and Tanya was offering it around with a gracious smile.

In the mad flurry to escape the monastery fire by leaping onto the back of a dragon, all their supplies and clothes had been left behind. The flask, however, she had somehow managed to rescue.

"It's like I dreamed you to life." Cassiel took a long drink, closing his eyes as the alcohol coursed fresh through his system. "The perfect woman..."

Two bright spots of color appeared on the shifter's cheeks, but she brushed it off with a casual grin. "Did all of that stuff really happen? Back in the djinn's tomb?"

"Oh, yes." Cassiel took one more drink before passing the flask off to Rose. "Vareezi venom is nothing to be trifled with. We were halfway back through the woods, when he became convinced I was going to strangle him. You should have heard the screams—"

"And that's enough story time." Dylan's eyes flickered self-consciously to Katerina before he gestured quickly to the others. "Tanya, why don't you get some wood for the fire? Rose, you can track down something for us to eat. And Cass, do a quick check of the perimeter."

His eyes flashed as they locked on the fae. "Unless, of course, you have more delightful stories to tell."

"Actually, I have a *lot* more stories—"

"*Cassiel.*"

The fae pushed to his feet with a smile. "I'm going, I'm going."

Within minutes the entire campsite was cleared out, leaving no one but Katerina and Dylan sitting together in the grass. He studied her for a moment, some uncertain emotion flickering in his eyes, before it settled into a tentative smile. "So, honey, huh?"

She shrugged her shoulders with a little grin. "It's better than puppy, don't you think?"

ROSE VOLUNTEERED TO take first watch that night. Ever since being allowed to depart with the others from Talsing, she seemed determined to prove herself. Determined to make up for lost time and earn her place amongst the gang. It wasn't the easiest group to break in to—and her aggressive sexuality didn't exactly help matters—but even Katerina had to admit that she was making progress.

"You're okay with Rose on lookout?" she asked curiously as she and Dylan settled down beside the fire. On the other side of the flames, Cassiel and Tanya were already fast asleep, nestled tight in each other's arms. "I mean, you're not going to try to sneak do it yourself?"

It was a fair question. The only person Dylan seemed completely at ease with keeping watch over the others was Cassiel. Whenever Tanya or Katerina were placed on lookout, it was only a matter of time before they found him lurking in the trees, casually watching over their shoulders.

At first, he'd tried to deny it. Blaming it on sleepwalking, or night terrors, or the classic 'I thought I heard something in the woods'. Those days had long since passed.

"Why? You're already tired of my company?"

Still wearing nothing beneath her thick cloak except an extra vest that Rose had found stuffed in her satchel, Katerina stifled a shiver. Instead, she glanced over her shoulder with a grin. "No. I just happen to know first-hand what an impossible control freak you are."

"Control freak?" He chuckled softly, slipping his arms casually around her waist. "I don't think anyone's ever called me that before."

Her lips curved up in a smirk. "Not to your face."

He laughed again and pulled her closer. So close that her shoulder blades were pressed right up against his ribs. She didn't think she'd ever get over it. The way they fit perfectly together. As if some higher power had designed them just so. Her head in the hollow of his shoulder. His chin resting lightly upon her hair. Hips pressed against hips. Legs entwined loosely together.

It was brand new, and yet there was the strangest sense of familiarity. Katerina didn't know how else to explain it. It felt like coming home.

"I really missed this," he said softly, whispering the words into her hair. "Holding you like this. Back at the monastery, I hated having separate rooms."

It never failed to surprise her when he said those sorts of things. His face was impossible to read under the best of circumstances, and half the time Katerina felt like the only place their relationship existed was inside her own head.

What relationship? a nagging voice piped up in the back of her mind. *You guys grab each other occasionally and make out. You love each other, but all that's over when you get back to the castle?*

If he felt her stiffen, he didn't let on. He simply bowed his head, pressing soft kisses into the back of her neck. A host of shivers ran down her spine, and she leaned back against him without realizing it. Reaching one hand up behind her to tangle in his hair. Suddenly wishing that his arms weren't outside the cloak but wrapped around her bare skin.

"Careful," he murmured, smiling against the back of her neck. "Don't make me do anything I can't take back in front of witnesses. I'll kill the others if I have to."

She glanced across the fire at Cassiel and Tanya's sleeping faces with a grin. No, if they were going to cross that line, it most certainly couldn't be tonight.

But you are going to cross it. Sooner or later... you know you are.

The realization settled over her all at once, lighting her up from the inside before leaving her suddenly cold. She'd often imagined her first time. Where would it be? Which nobleman would it be with? Would it be on her wedding night, or sometime sooner? She'd imagined roses and wine and candles. Horseback rides to midnight picnics where they made love under the stars. Over the course of the years, she'd imagined the scenario to have a little bit of everything.

But the one thing it didn't have was a deadline.

"What are we going to do?" she whispered. The warmth of his body seemed to have abruptly disappeared, leaving her cold and wanting. "How are we supposed to just put all this away the second we get back to my home? Are you just going to leave me there? I'll never see you again?"

His entire body went rigid as a board, then wilted with a quiet sigh. "I don't know, Katerina."

The kisses stopped. So did that hot pulse of longing. But the arms remained. His wrapped around her. Hers twined through his. Together, they held each other and gazed as one at the dying flames.

Each asking themselves the painful question.

Each at a loss as to the answer.

Until finally, at long last, they fell asleep.

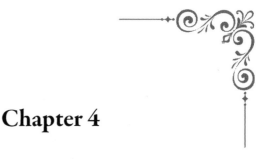

Chapter 4

Katerina jerked awake sometime after midnight. The fire had gone out, and despite Dylan's arms still wrapped around her she was unbearably cold. A violent shiver swept across her body, and although he squeezed automatically tighter in his sleep she slipped out from beneath him and pushed to her feet, driven by a restlessness she couldn't control.

The others were still dead asleep. Even the ever-vigilant Dylan had succumbed to fatigue. All of them content in the knowledge that Rose was still on lookout, keeping watch under the stars.

It's probably because she's a shifter; that's why he's okay with it, Katerina thought as she wandered away from the fire, setting out into the trees. *If anything happens, she can just wolf-out like him.*

A stab of jealousy shot through her before another voice piped up just as suddenly.

But you can shift, too. And into something a heck of a lot stronger than a wolf.

The thought both calmed and frightened her as she moved restlessly through the trees. At times, it was almost easy to forget. Like trying to remember a dream, or a story that had happened to someone else. Then, all of a sudden, it would hit her all over again.

After jumping off a cliff, she'd turned into a *dragon*. A real-life, fire-breathing dragon.

To be frank, she almost didn't know which was stranger: That dragons actually existed in real life, or that she had jumped willingly off the ledge instead of having tripped and fallen. One took a power she didn't know she had, and the other a bravery that had thus far eluded her. Yet, somehow, at no point during the entire experience had she felt remotely afraid.

I wonder if it was the same way for my mother. I wonder what she felt the first time it happened to her.

She wandered along with no thought as to distance or direction, winding her way through a shadowy wonderland of towering elms dripping with phosphorescent moss before coming out suddenly on the banks of the river. If possible, it was even more beautiful bathed in moonlight than it had been during the day. The light of the stars streaked the water with rippling waves of liquid silver, while the clusters of flowers on the other side were already misted with the faintest sheen of early-morning dew.

For a moment, Katerina simply stared. Her eyes, dazzled. Her mind, a million miles away.

Then she realized that someone was talking to her.

"Blink once if you can hear me." There was an expectant pause. "Okay, please tell me this is some kind of dragon meditation. That at any moment you could grow scales and take flight."

Katerina whipped around to see Rose watching her from on top of a nearby bluff. Her legs were folded up beneath her like a child, and there was a look of heightened anticipation in her eyes. The onyx was simmering with a deep curiosity, while the blue was sparking off energy like a bolt of lightning from the sky. Her fingers dug into the deep grass as she leaned forward with bated breath, like the princess was a powder keg just waiting to blow.

"No scales, I'm afraid." Katerina held up her arms with a guilty smile. "Just me."

The shifter flashed her a grin and patted the spot beside her, waiting patiently as the princess lifted Dylan's heavy cloak and made her way up the slippery hill. A moment or two later, they were both settled in the grass. Staring out over the lazily-flowing river.

It was a pleasant silence, but not an entirely comfortable one. No matter what strides the princess had made with Rose since her spontaneous apology by the bridge, there was still something undeniably intimidating about the girl. She was just as confident and outspoken as Tanya, but while there was a whimsical sweetness to the shape-shifter the wolf was still something of a mystery.

"Do you mind if I ask you something?" Katerina glanced sideways, out of the corner of her eye. She didn't miss the slight tensing of Rose's arms, still gripped tightly around her knees, but when she turned back to the princess her face had cleared with an easy smile.

"Shoot."

Katerina glanced down at her fingers for a moment, then met her steady gaze. "Why did you want to come with us when we left the monastery?" This time, the tension was much more palpable, and she hastened to explain. "It's just that, you don't know any of us very well and we're clearly on the run from some very dangerous people. Not to mention, I'm sure you went to Talsing in the first place for a reason..." She let her voice trail off, leaving the question floating in the air.

Rose considered it for a moment, appeared to be thinking very fast, then bowed her head with a sigh. "I *did* go to Talsing for a reason. I went there to get away from exactly the kind of people I saw were hunting you." Her voice was low and quick, not an ounce of bravado or pretense, unlike any tone she'd ever used before. "When I was sixteen years old, a battalion of infantrymen showed up out of nowhere and set fire to my village. They said they had come on royal orders to," her face screwed up with pure loathing as she repeated the exact quote, "to cleanse the land of the half-blood filth that had come to inhabit it."

Katerina flinched as though she'd been slapped and dropped her gaze back down to her palms. Yeah, that sounded like a royal decree all right.

"Not many of us made it out. The pack was strong, but the army was using shifters of their own. When the alpha fell, I knew things would never be the same. We ran for miles, but they were still hot on our trail. My mother just managed to get me out before she was killed herself. She told me to go to the Talsing Sanctuary. Said there was a man there who could help me. Said I'd be safe."

For a second, she looked very much like a child. Lost. Remote. Staring blankly into the abyss as the horrors of her past washed over her like a wave. Then those walls came right back up.

"I'm so sorry," Katerina murmured, still unable to meet her gaze. She might not have given the order herself, but that didn't mean she didn't know the people who did. She could picture the very room where it must have happened. "I don't even know what to say..."

The words lodged in a tender part of her brain, burrowing in deep and joining a whole host of troubles already nesting there. Virtually every person she'd met along the road thus far had shared a similar story. From a giant, to a shifter, to a fallen prince...all the way down to the maids who worked in the monastery kitchen.

All of them had been scorned by those people who had sworn to lead them. Their lives had been ripped apart by those people who should have been protecting them the most.

My family. My freakin' Damaris blood.

It felt like a living curse. Running hot and fast through her veins. No matter what she did, she could never be rid of it. No matter how much she tried to atone, it could never be made right.

"Your brother..."

Katerina lifted her head to see Rose watching her carefully. There was a look on her face that the princess had never seen before. A strange sort of caution she didn't understand.

"What about him?" she replied warily. Since leaving the castle, the princess had come to understand that conversations that started with 'Your brother' were seldom good.

Rose paused a moment, weighing her words, before she looked back up with that same intense curiosity. Like she was trying to fit the pieces together in a puzzle she'd never seen. "He really killed your father? Ran you out of the castle? Tried to kill you, too?"

It was a subject Katerina had done her best not to think about since leaving. Yes, it was always there in the back of her mind, like an open wound that could never seem to close, but every day since then had been so fraught with peril that she hadn't had much time to dwell on it.

But it was easy to think about now, with nothing to distract her but the quiet bubbling of the moonlit stream. In fact, it was impossible not to.

"He has these dogs," she said quietly, her eyes fixed on the dark bank of the river. "Twin hell hounds. He got them when we were kids." A faint shiver ran across her arms as she stared out into the darkness, half imagining she could see their yellow eyes. "He set them after me. They chased me all the way to the edge of the forest. If it wasn't for a cloaking spell, I wouldn't be here right now."

For a moment, Rose grew very still. Her eyes were wide as saucers, reflecting every stray bit of starlight as they gazed in wonder at the princess. Then a particular phrase seemed to strike home, and her face clouded as quickly as it had cleared.

"A spell?"

There was something strange in her voice, but Katerina was too distracted to notice. Too caught up reliving the memories she'd tried so hard to suppress.

"Yeah, a spell." She nodded quickly, trying to snap herself out of it. "There was a wizard back at the castle." She sighed. "Alwyn. He'd looked after me since I was a child. On the night of my father's murder he did a cloaking spell, so I could sneak out unharmed. He's actually the one who told me to go to Talsing," she added suddenly. "To keep me safe. Kind of like your mom."

A look of pure rage flitted across the shifter's face, but it was gone before either girl could register it. Vanishing back into the shadows of the night.

"Wizards can be tricky." Rose pressed her lips tight. "We were always told to stay away from them as children, as it's said they bring nothing but trouble."

Katerina glanced sideways but said nothing. It wasn't exactly an uncommon warning. Going all the way back to the Middle Ages, wizards had always been feared for their immense power. She was just lucky she'd found one of the good ones.

"Shouldn't you be waking Cass?" Katerina asked abruptly, changing the subject. The moon had risen high in the sky, and it was surely past her appointed time of watch. "You're going to want to get some rest before morning. I'm sure Dylan will have us on the war path all over again."

A burst of quiet laughter broke the silence as both girls lay back on the grass, propping themselves up on their elbows and thinking back on the events of the day.

"Naw, I'm good right here," Rose finally replied. "Probably best if I give him and Tanya a wide berth for a while anyway. Let things cool down."

Katerina snorted and shook her head. "That's your own fault, you know. Why do you always have to be so—"

"—endearing?"

The princess laughed again. "I was going to say intrusive."

Rose shrugged, flashing a pearly smile as the midnight breeze played with the ends of her dark hair. "There's no harm in just looking, is there? And on that note," she flipped suddenly onto her side, staring at Katerina, "what are *you* doing out here?"

Katerina stiffened automatically, as if her inner monologue about both Dylan and her mother had been playing out loud. "What do you mean?"

"If I was curled up with Dylan Aires, I'd stay there no matter what." Rose tossed back her hair with a brazen grin. "You couldn't drag me away—dragon or not."

A nervous smile flitted across Katerina's face, but she found herself suddenly unable to talk about why exactly it was so difficult to be around Dylan at the moment. Much less to someone so obviously willing to try to steal him away. Instead, she tried to play the whole thing off. "I just couldn't sleep," she answered with a casual shrug. "Thought I might go for a walk, try to find a snack or something."

Rose's face lit up as she pushed to her feet, offering a hand to Katerina in the same fluid motion. Shifters were unexpectedly graceful like that. It was a quality that had made the princess deeply jealous when she saw it in the others. A part of her wondered if she'd start to develop it now herself. She took Rose's hand and got to her feet.

"There was a cluster of fruit trees just a bit down the river," the shifter explained, pointing a slender arm down the sparkling shore. "I was going to get something for myself. A quick bite, then we'll both head back to camp?"

Katerina followed her gaze and nodded. Pleased that she'd let the subject drop instead of pressing for more information. It was one of the best things about Rose—she didn't press.

"Yeah, sounds perfect."

Together, the two of them left the bank behind and headed down to the water. It was more turbulent the farther they walked, stirring up into a milky froth as they headed towards the falls. The mixture of sand and smooth stones crunched under Katerina's bare feet, and she thanked whatever higher power was looking out for them that the path they'd taken had been forgiving of the fact that she no longer had any shoes. She suspected that was why Dylan had chosen the lower trail that took them through the valley. That 'higher power' looking out for her usually turned out to be him.

As if reading her mind, Rose flashed her a sudden grin. "We're going to have to get you some boots in the next town we stop in. Probably some pants, too."

Katerina chuckled and pulled the cloak instinctively tighter as memories of Dylan's and her early- morning tryst flashed through her mind. "Yeah, pants would be good."

Rose nixed the first few trees they passed, claiming that plums 'tasted like death,' before coming to a sudden stop in front of a trio of bushes with thick, glossy leaves. Under each leaf was a cluster of brightly-colored berries. Plump and red and dangling invitingly in the silver light.

"Oh, perfect," Rose grabbed a handful and eased them gently off the stem. "Night bloom."

"Night bloom?" Katerina repeated curiously. If the shifter hadn't stopped she would never have noticed the bushes, which were darker and set slightly away from the rest. She certainly would never have thought to look underneath the thick leaves. "What's that?"

"Best berries in the world." Rose handed what she'd picked to Katerina and turned to get some more for herself. "My grandmother used to bake them in pies."

The princess nodded absentmindedly and popped the first one into her mouth. It exploded the second her teeth pierced it, dissolving in a burst of the sweetest juice she'd ever tasted. Without thinking, she popped in another. Then another after that.

"These are incredible!" She licked the purple stain off the tips of her fingers. "We've got to bring some back for the others. I can't believe we haven't... we haven't picked some... before..."

Her voice trailed away as the picture in front of her suddenly changed.

Had the colors always been so bright? The silver-teal of the water. The rich emerald hue of the forest trees. Even the amethyst stain of the berries leaching into her porcelain skin. She stared for a moment in absolute wonder, lifting her hand in front of her face and turning it back and forth.

Her legs wanted to give out beneath her. For a moment, she thought they had. They were tingling so pleasantly she didn't know how they could possibly support her. But when she glanced down, they were still planted upon the grass swaying slightly in the breeze. She was about to touch them just to make sure, but she got distracted again by the sight of her hands.

It was strange that people even had hands. Why didn't they walk on four legs, like the rest of the animals? She'd certainly enjoyed it as a dragon. Not that she'd needed legs. All she'd needed as a dragon was the horizon, the whisper of the wind, the wide-open night sky...

"Katerina?"

She was moving now, though she didn't remember deciding to do so. A feeling of surreal weightlessness tickled through her limbs as she floated down the river bank and towards the rushing falls below. Never before had she seen such beauty. The way the water swirled and coiled as it eddied around the rocks. The way it flew out with abandon over the granite cliff before exploding into mist down in the little pool, hundreds of feet below.

Magical. Everything here is magical.

Katerina's arms drifted out from her sides as she stepped a foot into the icy water.

...even me.

"Kat, what are you doing?"

A serene smile spread across her face as she made her way over the smooth stones. A tug of current pulling her forward. Dylan's cloak trailing in the surf behind her like a watery cape. A shower of mist sprayed up around her, and the light of the moon dazzled her eyes.

Just a little further. You're almost there.

Even at the top of the falls the raging tide only came up to her knees, but it wasn't the water she was concerned with. Neither was she concerned with the sound of distant shouting, or that the world around her had gone suddenly still. Her mind was focused, and her body was centered upon a single thing. A solitary desire that filled every bit of open space, until she thought she might burst if she didn't have it. Her toes curled around the edge of the cliff as she lifted her arms into the air.

It's such a good night for flying...

With that she closed her eyes, tilted her face to the moon with a beatific smile, and leapt with a feeling of pure euphoria over the edge of the falls.

Chapter 5

All the air smacked out of Katerina's body in one harsh blow. Leaving her lungs wilted and her mouth gasping for breath. She had time only to glance up in wonder. To marvel at the fierce beauty of his frightened face. Then she tumbled back into icy darkness and all was quiet once more.

Maybe not such a good night for flying after all.

Strong arms were tugging her against the current. Fighting their way to shore. Her head broke out of the water and that sweet air that had eluded her thus far went tearing, cold and sharp, down her throat. She coughed up what felt like a river of half-frozen water, her head rolling limply as her arms dragged by her sides, but still she was moving forward. Held safely above the water.

Her eyes cracked open and little bits of light started piercing through. Not the bright light of morning, as the world was still cloaked in darkness, but softer light. Moonlight and a velvety curtain of stars. She tried to focus on just one thing. Tried to make sense of what was going on around her, but it was no use. Her head was spinning, and her body felt as though it had been ripped in half.

A part of her was desperate for the air, grateful for the rescue, but another part was still standing on the edge of the cliff—arms out, awash with euphoria as she tried to take flight.

"Lemme go," she mumbled, struggling weakly against the arms. "I'ave tago back."

The arms tightened as Dylan doubled his speed. She could feel his heart thumping through the wet fabric that clung to his chest. How his muscles went taut as a violent shiver rippled across his skin. He was panting, that much she could tell, but if he answered she was unable to hear it.

"Lemme go," she said again, a bit stronger than before. "I want to fly."

This time there was no mistaking the snort of derision that tightened his shoulders. The way his hands hoisted her higher against his body as he tugged her back to shore.

"So that's it, huh?" he breathed, his voice only barely louder than the rushing waves crashing into mist in the distance. "That's why I found you standing on the edge of a freaking cliff—ready to jump. *Again*. You wanted to fly?"

She tried to answer. Tried to make some kind of case for herself. But she was exhausted to the core and her head fell back against him, wet hair wrapping around his wrist like fiery seaweed. "...pretty." She lifted a shaking hand, pointing up at the stars. When he turned to look the moonlight spilled across his high cheekbones, and long shadows from his wet lashes spilled down the edges of his face. Her lips curved up in a smile. "So are you."

For the first time since he'd tackled her, that look of concern melted into one of surprise. An eyebrow lifted incredulously, but before he could say a word another wave of current hit them and he braced his feet hard against the slick stone, bending forward as he fought against the water.

"Seven hells," he muttered as they inched forward. "Only you..."

The others were gathered on the shore by now; Katerina could see them over the ridge of Dylan's arm. Rose was standing with them, but her face was shock-white. One hand kept drifting up, as if she was answering a question at school, while the other clutched the shirt above her heart.

Cassiel shouted something in what had to be a dialect of the fae, but Dylan just shook his head. They were already coming up out of the river; he didn't need any help.

Up close, they looked just as scared as he was. And more than a little confused.

"Is she okay?" Tanya demanded once they got within range. "Dylan, is she okay?"

I must look pretty bad if they're not even addressing their questions to me.

Dylan nodded, but he seemed rather incapable of speech himself. And even though he'd just battled tooth and nail against the current to bring her back, Katerina didn't think the uncharacteristic quiet had anything to do with fatigue. It went far deeper than that. Right down to his core.

The second they were back on dry land, he set her down gently. But her legs gave out immediately beneath her and he caught her again in surprise, cradling her delicately in his arms.

"Kat," he said quietly, giving her a gentle shake, "are you all right?"

She stared up at him but couldn't remember any of the right words.

"Say something, babe. Talk to me."

This time, just staring wasn't enough. She lifted a hand to his face with that same wide-eyed wonder she'd had before. Running it along the side of his cheek and marveling at the texture. It wasn't until a stream of water dripped into her eyes that she pulled back with sudden concern. "You're all wet," she said in surprise. "What happened to you?"

Rose made a half-strangled sound as Dylan stared down in astonishment. A full thirty seconds passed before he reached out suddenly and caught her by the hand.

"What's this?" He looked down at the blood-red stain on the tips of her fingers. "Did you cut yourself on something?"

Before she could even answer he began checking her over for wounds, but she pushed his hands away, muttering something that sounded like 'berries.'

"Berries?" he repeated, slowly putting it together. His eyes traveled once more from her stained fingers, to where Rose stood cowering behind the others, before narrowing with sudden ferocity. "What berries did she eat? What did you do to her?"

He's blaming Rose?

Katerina sat up in surprise—or, at least, she tried to. Moving was a little difficult at the moment. So was ungluing her tongue from the roof of her mouth. So was taking her eyes off Dylan.

He looked like a furious prince. Haloed by a crown of stars.

...soooo very pretty.

"What did you give her?" he demanded again before Rose could open her mouth to reply. It looked as though he would have shifted right then and there if he hadn't still been holding Katerina.

"Just that," Rose answered breathlessly, pointing to the bushes the two had plundered what felt like just moments before. "Night bloom. I've had it ever since I was a child..."

She trailed off as Dylan placed the princess securely in Cassiel's arms and stormed over to investigate himself. Katerina watched with wide eyes, trying to keep up with the conversation as he pulled off a berry and gave it a cursory glance. A second later, his face tightened with rage.

"This isn't night bloom." His fist closed around it, leaking giant crimson drops onto the ground. "It's banewort—a bloody hallucinogen! In large doses, it can be fatal!"

Rose's mouth fell open in despair, but she shook her head desperately. "I didn't know! It looks so much like—"

"How many did she have?" Dylan demanded.

"She only had three!"

This, at least, seemed to pacify him. He swept back to Cassiel at once and took the princess once again, lowering her gently to the grass. "You're going to be okay," he soothed, stroking back her wet hair. But every few seconds his eyes would lift to Rose in a deadly glare.

"I'm so sorry," the shifter murmured, taking a step back and shaking from head to toe. "The second I saw something was wrong I ran to get you..."

Dylan didn't answer. He merely continued with his silent reassurances as the others moved forward to examine the plant for themselves. Tanya had been just as indignant as him, but she softened when she saw the bushes.

"Dylan, this looks exactly like night bloom."

He flashed her the same glare before returning to Katerina. But even Cassiel rubbed the leaves briefly between his fingers, shaking his head.

"They are incredibly close," he said softly. "Even I might have taken some."

"No. You wouldn't have," Dylan snapped, clutching Katerina closer to his chest as he leveled Rose with a terrifying glare. "This is what happens when I leave you in charge. The first night you're ever on watch and look what happens."

"Dylan, that's not fair," Tanya interceded quietly. "It was a mistake. You wouldn't blame me if I'd been the one on lookout."

"You would never have been so careless!" There wasn't an ounce of leniency in his voice as he turned back to Rose; it was as hard and cold as steel. "You have no idea what's at stake here! You have no idea how important she is! What she means to...to everyone!"

The others glanced down at their feet, and even Katerina had the wherewithal to realize that Dylan had made some kind of mistake. He glanced away, the tops of his cheeks coloring with a faint blush as Rose trembled and backed shamefully towards the camp.

"I'm sorry," she whispered again and again. "I'm so sorry..."

Tanya shot Dylan an exasperated glare and headed after her while Cassiel knelt down beside the two who remained, slipping off his cloak and laying it across Katerina's shivering body.

"You should build a fire," he advised softly. "Get her dry and warm. She might not feel it now, but her skin's already like ice."

Is it? Katerina tried to think about it objectively. *Am I cold right now? Is that why I'm shivering?*

"So is yours," Cassiel continued with a slight warning, pushing to his feet and eyeing his friend with concern. "You're soaked to the bone, Dylan. Take care of yourself, too."

Dylan nodded distractedly, but his eyes never left Katerina's face. "I will."

There was a slight pause.

"*Dylan.*"

"Yeah." He finally broke eye contact, giving Cassiel an obedient nod. "I will. I swear."

Cassiel nodded swiftly, then vanished into the trees. Leaving Katerina alone with Dylan at last. Lying in his arms as the two shivered in silence on the peaceful riverbank. Finally, when it could go on no longer, he let out a sigh, stroking a long finger down the side of her face.

"What am I going to do with you?" he murmured, shaking his head.

She blinked up at him before her face transformed with a breathtaking smile. "I think I know why people have two hands."

His lips twitched, and he bowed his head. "Well, at least we've got *that* settled."

THE REST OF THE NIGHT might have felt like ages to Dylan, but it passed by in the blink of an eye to Katerina. As the hours ticked on, she amused herself in any of a number of ways. Trying desperately and persistently to braid his hair. Weeping loudly when she wasn't allowed.

Curling up as close as she could to the fire before becoming abruptly frightened of the dancing flames. Then she wanted to touch the flames. When Dylan didn't let her, she tried to make flames of her own.

All in all, it was shaping up to be a brilliant night. She didn't even realize she was naked.

"Would you stop doing that?" Dylan shook his head with an amused exasperation, catching the cloak she'd tried tossing onto the fire and draping it back across her body. "You know, any minute now you're going to snap out of it. And you're going to be pretty damn pissed that I let you take your clothes off when you do."

Katerina wriggled uncomfortably under the heavy fabric, longing to rip it off once more. "I'm hot."

He chuckled silently, drawing her closer up to his chest. "You're not hot, honey. Just a second ago, you were telling me that you were cold."

"Compromise!" Her face lit up and she twisted around to face him, thrilled with her own brilliance. "Half in, half out!"

Before he could stop her, she ripped off the cloak once more. This time, however, she only pulled it down to her waist, curling into his chest with a satisfied smile. "There. Perfect."

Dylan was too stunned to speak. He'd been having that problem a lot lately. Ever since Rose came bursting back into the campsite, shrieking about how the princess was going to jump. That, at least, he could handle. A midnight rescue? A last-second tackle on the edge of a cliff? That was child's play. But this? A beautiful, naked woman curling up in his arms? He was at a loss for words.

"Do you think birds dream?"

The moment shattered, and he laughed again, circling his arms tentatively around her bare back. Her skin was just as soft as he'd imagined. He stroked his thumb along her spine. "I think they probably do. I think most things dream."

She paused for a moment, considering this. Then her face screwed up with a frown. "What about catfish?"

His teeth sank into his lower lip as he tried to keep from laughing. Or cursing. Or any of a number of other things that crossed his mind as he stared down at her naked flesh. "Definitely not," he answered decisively. "Catfish do not dream."

She blinked up at him, then nodded. Apparently satisfied. Even though her back was now to the fire, the glow of it still lit her skin. Like a fiery halo. A flaming caress that silhouetted the gentle curves of her body and made her eyes dance like little jewels.

"You're so beautiful," he murmured before he could stop himself. "Sometimes I don't...I don't know what to do with myself around you."

It was hard to tell whether the words had taken effect. Over the last few hours, she'd drifted in and out of their current reality. Sometimes, she was alert and responsive. Other times, she was in her own little world. Right now, she seemed to be somewhere in between.

Or maybe not...

Without breaking eye contact for a moment, without saying a single word, she took his hand and placed it deliberately on her body. Right in the delicate hollow of her neck. His breath caught in his chest, and for a moment he thought about resisting. Then he let her slowly guide him down the length of her side. Past her ribcage, along the edge of her waist. She pressed him on to go further, but he stopped suddenly when he reached the gentle curve of her hip.

"Katerina... I can't."

She didn't seem fazed by this one way or another. She simply stared up at him. Vulnerable and trusting. Those eyes like little diamonds sparkling in the light of the moon.

"You don't want to?"

For a split second, he almost laughed. Did he not *want* to? He had never heard a more ridiculous question. YES, he wanted to. More than anything. It was hard to think of anything else when he was walking beside her, day after day. Sleeping beside her, night after night.

He almost laughed, but the look on her face kept him silent. Then, at the sight of his hand still resting tentatively on his skin, every thought of laughter died.

"You're high."

One way or another, he couldn't have this moment with her. Not unless she was fully aware of what was happening. Of the weight of what she was asking. Not two minutes ago, they'd been discussing the nocturnal habits of catfish. She was in no state now to be making this decision.

"High?" She repeated the word carefully, like she was testing it out. "I suppose I am." A second later, her face lit up with a mischievous smile. "Do you want to be high, too?"

This time there was no holding back the laughter. It rang out between them, loud and clear, as Dylan tilted his head back to the stars. "No. I think one of us should probably stay grounded."

"Oh, come on." Without a word of warning she rolled onto his chest, knocking him flat on his back with a grin. "I could find some more berries. They taste really good."

Her smile remained, but his own had abruptly frozen. It was one thing when she was half-covered, huddled safely out of sight in his arms. It was another entirely when she was lying on top of him, the cloak in a forgotten pile on the ground, her crimson hair cascading onto his chest.

He pulled in a sharp breath, the inside of his mouth going suddenly dry. "What are you doing to me?"

She cocked her head to the side, like an adorably contemplative angel. "...tempting you with berries?"

There was a pause.

"No, I meant—"

He broke off with a breathless chuckle, shaking his head. How were you supposed to explain it? Especially to someone high on hallucinogens.

"Never mind." He ran his hands down along the length of her body, stopping when he got to the small of her back. He was painfully aware of the way every electrified cell in his body was standing on end. He was painfully aware of her involuntary shiver. "Listen, we should probably—"

A twig snapped behind them and his entire body froze dead still. A second later he was on his feet, the princess huddled in the cloak behind him, his hand reaching desperately for his blade.

...a blade that he'd left back at the camp.

"Who's there?" he called out a lot more bravely than he felt. Wishing he was still wearing a shirt. Hoping like hell that Cassiel would hear his voice and come running. "Show yourself!"

For a split second, all was quiet. Then there was a slight rustling in the trees. Dylan watched with bated breath as the foliage parted and out stepped half a dozen grizzled faces. Half a dozen faces that he'd seen many times before. Quite recently, in fact.

"Craston?"

The sturdy dwarf stepped into the light with a broad grin, stroking his red beard as the rest of his companions piled into the clearing along with him.

"I see you decided not to ransom the girl after all." His twinkling eyes swept Katerina up and down, lingering with great appreciation. "But you did find a good way to pass the time..."

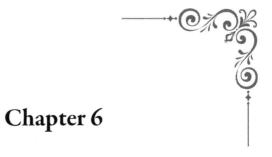

Chapter 6

C *raston.*

The word was enough to break through to Katerina. Penetrating the deep mental fog and dragging her slowly back to the light. The last time she'd heard the name, she'd been huddled on the ground. Freezing. Wrapped in a cloak. Waiting for a band of little men to decide her fate.

Looking around now, it seemed as though her circumstances had scarcely improved.

"Dylan," she whispered, unaware that she was probably speaking a bit louder than she should, "you're going to have to fight them. I'll create a diversion. You take the big ugly one in front."

The 'big ugly one in front' looked at her curiously before turning back to Dylan, his eyes twinkling in the light of the fire. "What the heck's wrong with her?"

"Banewort," Dylan replied simply as he moved Katerina's cloak to cover her shoulders. "It's been like this all night."

The dwarf chuckled. A deep rumbling laugh that seemed to start all the way down in his belly. "Well, you seemed to have been making good use of the time."

The others joined the laughter while Dylan bristled defensively.

"I wasn't going to do anything," he said a little sharply, crossing his arms self-consciously over his bare chest. It was only then Katerina realized he wasn't wearing a shirt. "What are you doing here anyway? Shouldn't you be off mining something? Playing around in the dirt?"

It was an old stereotype, one that stopped the laughter in its tracks. Only Dylan's long history with the group and his comical situation allowed him to keep his head.

"Still smarting off, I see." Craston shook his head with an indulgent smile. "And never more so than when you're vastly outnumbered and missing a shirt. Some things never change."

Even Dylan had to smile at that one, although Katerina was still completely lost. A vague part of her was saying that this was probably okay, that Dylan would be more agitated if these odd little men meant them any harm. But another part was still held firmly in the grip of the berries.

With what she took to be the greatest discretion she eased away from him, reaching down towards the rim around the fire to pick up a large rock.

If he's not going to fight them, I'll just have to do it myself.

As the dwarves and the ranger struck up a friendly conversation the rock came up slowly behind her head, gripped tight in her fist. She was feeling pretty good about her chances, ready to take them all out with a single throw, when a pair of cool fingers closed around her wrist. Her head jerked up in surprise only to see Cassiel standing in the darkness behind her, a soft moonlit glow illuminating the affectionate smile on his face.

"That's not the best way to make friends." He pried gently the rock loose and let it drop to the ground between them. It was only then he noticed her attire—or, rather, the lack thereof. She'd apparently forgotten to close the cloak. "But *that's* a nice way to start." A flicker of confusion splashed across his face, then he glanced suddenly between her and Dylan. "Tell me you didn't—"

"There he is! The prince of the fair folk himself!" Craston stepped forward with a wide smile, arms extended, seeing the fae for the first time. "Cass, good to see you, old friend."

Cassiel stepped forward with a grin, bending low to share an embrace before flashing a smile at the rest of the gang. Whatever history Dylan had with these people the fae obviously had it, too.

"And still saving this one, I see." Craston jerked his head back towards the ranger with a little smirk. "Tell me, does it ever get tiring?"

It wasn't often their fearless leader got picked on and, despite her present mental state, Katerina was greatly enjoying it now. Dylan—not so much. His eyes cooled with a wry expression as Cassiel and Craston shared a laugh.

"Kids will be kids," the fae answered with a theatrical smile. Although he and Dylan looked on the outside to be the same age, it was sometimes easy to forget that Cassiel was more than eighty years older. "You leave them alone for one second—"

"And they end up tricking some lovely maiden into bed," Craston finished with a grin.

Cassiel's smile faded slightly, and he shot Dylan a hard look. "Yes, it seems they do."

Katerina was beginning to get suspicious that she was the maiden in question. Her eyes widened, and she stared at the men in shock, unable to believe what she was seeing. Cassiel was feeling *protective*? Of *her*? Against *Dylan*? Did wonders never cease?

"I didn't," Dylan said in a hushed undertone, taking the fae's accusatory look to heart and desperate for his friend to understand. "Nothing happened—"

"So, where are you headed?" Craston interrupted cheerfully.

Whatever tension had sprung up between the ranger and the fae, none of the dwarves seemed to notice. They were a blunt kind of people. Taking great pride in being plainspoken and steadfast as a rock. The subtler nuances of more human behavior seldom troubled them.

Dylan paused for a moment before deciding to go with the truth. "We're heading up to the camp at Pora. Maybe afterwards to the one in Rorque."

The dwarf lifted his bushy eyebrows, taken aback. "Is that so?" A faint hush of conversation whispered through his companions, but he kept his eyes locked on Dylan. "Back to that old game? I thought it was all behind you."

Cassiel tensed and Dylan shook his head briskly, looking a bit sorry that he hadn't decided to lie after all. "Not just yet."

The dwarf nodded slowly, stroking a hand down the entire length of his crimson beard in a thoughtful manner. "And this little trip of yours to Pora...it wouldn't have anything to do with the news we just heard of a royal battalion vanishing up near the Talsing Sanctuary, would it?"

There was a beat of silence.

Then Dylan flashed a charming smile. "Lucky coincidence."

Craston grunted his disbelief before turning to Cassiel, the voice of reason. "You okay with this?"

"Not remotely," the fae answered immediately. "But I'm... coming along."

This part of the story made sense.

Katerina remembered her first encounter with Craston, where he and his friends had dragged her out of bed in the hopes of ransoming her off to the highest bidder. He'd asked Dylan then what he was doing so far south, surprised that he was no longer rousing the rebels. Of course, Dylan had cut him off before he could say as much, trying to keep the awkward piece of information away from Katerina.

Yes, this part of the story made sense.

The princess could tell that the dwarves were hardly surprised to see the two young friends throwing themselves back into the heart of the rebellion. It was in Dylan's nature to go. It was in Cassiel's nature to protect him. The only piece of the puzzle that didn't seem to fit was her.

"My dear, I don't believe we were ever properly introduced." Craston slowly made his way towards her, eyes twinkling with a hundred questions as he held out his hand. "Craston Overlarq of the Den Mareen. These are my humble subjects."

The rest of them did an unintentionally choreographed wave, like something out of a child's book, while Katerina's wide eyes fixed upon Craston's face.

No. They had not been 'properly introduced.' Not unless you counted kidnapping and the fact that he'd slapped her across the face. She didn't feel inclined to be 'properly introduced' now.

"You're lucky I don't set you on fire."

Cassiel lifted his eyes to the heavens while Dylan swept hastily in between them, looking scandalized. "*Katerina!*"

Under most circumstances, she would have held her tongue. But the berries had given her courage to speak her mind and eroded lingering inhibitions that might have stood in her way.

Self-preservation being one of them.

"I'm sorry," Dylan apologized swiftly, shooting Craston a penitent look as he simultaneously pulled Katerina several steps away. "It's the damn berries. She doesn't know what she's saying."

"Yes, I do," Katerina insisted, glaring daggers at the grizzled little man. "And I wouldn't feel sorry about it, either. You lot would smoke up like little briskets."

Little briskets? In hindsight, it was most unfortunate she'd selected that particular word.

Dylan's face paled and he clapped a hand over her mouth. Cassiel tensed so dramatically she could feel the tension rolling off of him from several feet away. Every buck-toothed smile abruptly melted off the dwarves, and when Craston took a step forward he looked positively terrifying.

"Light me on fire, huh? Smoke me up like a brisket?"

Dylan's hand tightened, but Katerina still managed to sneer through his fingers.

"You're just lucky I'm feeling benevolent."

For a moment, all was quiet. Then Craston let loose a laugh so wild she felt the vibrations of it shaking through the ground at her feet. A moment after that, his companions all joined in.

"Benevolent?" The dwarf actually had tears in his eyes. This from a people who weren't exactly prone to emotions. "Yes, I suppose it's lucky that you are."

Cassiel's face relaxed ever so slightly with a nervous smile. Dylan still looked like he was about to throw up. But the dwarves were having none of it. Without another word, Craston threw his arm around the ranger's shoulder—more like his chest—and began leading them all away.

"Come, friend. Tonight, we'll share a camp. Tell me more about this journey of yours." His eyes twinkled as they flashed back to Katerina. "And tell me more about this girl..."

BY THE TIME THEY GOT back to where Tanya and Rose were resting, the power of the berries was beginning to fade. Katerina still felt the lingering grip of their influence—that sly little voice in the back of her head, telling her stupid things to do—but she kept perfectly silent. Leaning against Dylan's side, the lot of them settled down around the campfire. Listening with wide eyes as the smoke spiraled up into the forest, the flask was passed around and the stories started to fly.

"—which is exactly when Dylan here decided that he'd had enough of the magistrate one way or another." Great big tears were streaming from Craston's eyes as he rolled back with laughter, clutching his flagon of mead. "Slipped a loop of rope around his ankle, the other side was tied to his horse. Slapped the horse on the rump and the thing took off running, dragging the king's 'royal ambassador' right out of town. I've never seen anything like it. Kid was only sixteen."

The others burst out laughing, while Dylan flushed and looked down with a grin. As much as the man teasingly boasted about himself, he seemed genuinely uncomfortable when other people did it. It was a strike against him in this crowd.

"Wasn't that the same week we raided the royal supply line?" another dwarf with black-cropped hair and beady eyes piped up suddenly. He flashed Dylan a conspiratorial grin. "The one where you ever so graciously volunteered to distract the corporal's daughter?"

The crowd burst out laughing again, while Dylan shot Katerina a stricken look. One that didn't entirely hide his blush. "That wasn't what you think. It wasn't fun for me."

Katerina lifted her eyebrows and folded her arms firmly across her chest. "And why not?"

The blush deepened and the dwarves around them roared until they cried.

"She was a Vendrosi," he mumbled. "Had six arms. It was a little... overwhelming."

The laughter reached new heights just as Cassiel returned, dumping an armful of logs atop the fire. "What are we talking about?"

Craston handed him a glass of mead. "The perils and pitfalls of a Vendrosi maid..."

"Vendrosi?" Cassiel's face brightened. "I love the Vendrosi!"

Of course, he did.

Tanya shot him a dangerous look, while Dylan tried to steer the conversation back on course. "Yeah, yeah, we all go back a long way." His face sobered as he leaned towards Craston, across the fire. "So, what brings *you* to these parts? Why aren't you home with Bruella?"

"Home with Bruella? Bruella's gone," Craston replied. The smile faded from his face as he stared into the bottom of his empty glass. "All the women and children are. They went underground the second the regiment at Talsing caught fire. The prince is on the warpath. Calling in all his bannermen. Something about finding his missing sister..."

For the second time, his eyes swept over Katerina. But there was no judgement in them. No accusation. Just a sparkle of curiosity. A silent question waiting for a reply.

A reply that the little group of friends was unable to give. Tanya and Rose stiffened defensively with identical looks of fear. Cassiel leaned casually forward, half-blocking Katerina from view. And Dylan, who had retrieved both his shirt and weapon since returning to camp, met the dwarf's gaze evenly—hand upon his blade.

But Craston wasn't looking at him. He was only looking at Katerina.

"They say the men all burned at Talsing," he continued quietly, his gruff voice growing unexpectedly gentle. "That fire rained down from the sky." He and the princess locked eyes. "It seems someone wasn't feeling so benevolent then."

There was a heavy pause. Then Katerina inclined her head. "No," she replied softly, "someone wasn't."

So, there it was. The deadly secret. The one they'd all guarded so zealously. It was finally out in the open. There for the entire world to see.

When she and Dylan had first set out on their dangerous quest, he'd told her that they would tell people who she was. The right people. At the right time. A time when she would be safe. But she had grown up in the weeks that had followed. Learned to see the error in his words. To peel away the protective gauze and see the world for what it really was.

She would never be safe. Not as long as Kailas lived. Not as long as those dogs stood at his side. Not as long as the army was under his control.

It was time to start trusting people. It was time to take a chance.

Dylan had said not a word to help her, but he'd done nothing to stop her either. He was giving her the choice. Prepared to stand by her either way. Craston, however, was on the fence.

"There are a thousand reasons that I should kill you on the spot," he said practically. "A thousand lives that demand personal retribution."

There was a quiet rumbling through the dwarves, and Katerina remembered Dylan saying how they'd be tough to fight. But, as luck would have it, a fight was not what the night had in store.

"But, seeing you here with Aires," Craston continued, "after all he's tried to do... it makes me wonder." His eyes flashed to Dylan before returning to Katerina. "Whose side are you on?"

The princess straightened up and looked him right in the eyes. "I'm with the *people*."

It was the exact right thing to say. And, under the circumstances, there was a good chance that she and all her friends would have ended up dead if she hadn't said exactly that. The faint rumbling through the ranks of the dwarves was replaced with a sudden hush as they all turned towards Craston—waiting for him to render his judgement.

"You were heading east?" Dylan asked quietly, cocking his head back to the trees. "The tracks you made. You were heading east?"

Craston nodded, never taking his eyes off the princess. "Yes."

There was a pause, then the ranger lifted his bright eyes.

"I couldn't persuade you to head north?"

Another pause. One during which people on both sides held their breath.

"Persuade me? With this crew?" Craston's eyes flickered around the campfire before wrinkling with the hint of a smile. "Yes... I think I could be persuaded."

THE NEWLY EXPANDED company was set to leave early the next morning, but Katerina's body was in no shape to do so. Her head felt like it weighed a thousand pounds, her tongue was thick and dry, and no matter how many times she blinked it was like her eyes couldn't manage to adjust to the bright morning light.

"Hey there, sleepyhead."

She sat up stiffly on her blanket—courtesy of the dwarves—and saw Dylan kneeling in front of her, an amused smile on his handsome face. In one hand, he held a bowl of what looked like a lumpy kind of porridge. In the other, a wad of clothes. They were approximately the same color.

"It's a good thing you're so tiny," he said with a grin. "It looks like some of Wallington's extra clothes might actually fit you."

Wallington?

Katerina lifted her head as an especially toothy dwarf waved to her from across the campsite. She lifted a hand automatically as her face crinkled with a frown. "Extra clothes?"

She reached for the fabric instead of the porridge, flipping it open to see a surprisingly-gender-neutral blouse and trousers. It would certainly be wide around the middle, but it was nothing that she couldn't fix with a little belt or piece of twine.

"We couldn't very well have you going around naked, could we?" Dylan cocked his head mischievously towards the dwarves. "Not in this lot."

The words awakened a suppressed memory in Katerina, dragging it forth out of the hallucinogenic bliss where it had been hiding. She froze for a second, trying to recall anything that had happened the previous night, then her face blanched to the color of sour milk.

Naked. I was very, very naked last night.

Dylan seemed to realize his mistake at the same time and he flashed her a quick, panicked look before dropping his eyes to the ground. "Kat, I just wanted you to know that I didn't..." He trailed off, at a loss for words. "I would never have let things get away from us when you were..."

"Dylan," Rose called from across the clearing. "Craston wants you."

He pushed abruptly to his feet, leaving behind the porridge and looking wildly relieved that he'd been spared that particular conversation. It wasn't until he was already several steps away that he glanced back uncertainly.

"So, we're... I mean, you and me... we're—"

Katerina started nodding so fast she thought her head might fall off. "We're good."

He ducked his head with a jerking nod, then vanished at a fast pace into the crowd. At this rate, he might just end up forgiving Rose after all. Katerina stared after him for a moment, too beside herself to speak, then looked down at the clothes in her hand.

Where were you yesterday, Wallington? I needed you.

She was about to get up and find some secluded spot where she could get dressed unnoticed, when another dwarf plopped down on the blanket beside her. This one was a little smaller than the rest. Almost scrawny. He looked younger, too. The deep lines edging the sides of his rather unattractive face hadn't yet begun to settle.

"What a bloody day!" he exclaimed, letting out all his breath in one angry burst. "First, I found a tear in the sheath for my dagger, then I couldn't get my hair to stay down, then I realized that all the rest of the whiskey has been officially 'rationed out' for the entire group." His beetle eyes flashed pure murder. "It's not even nine in the morning, and I already want to kill everyone!"

Katerina stared on in shock, at a complete loss for words.

What in seven hells is happening right now?

After a few seconds of silence, the dwarf shot her a casual look. "I see that you got some clothes. Want me to hold up my cloak or something so you can change?"

Excuse me?

"No!" Katerina exclaimed, pushing to her feet. The dwarf looked up in surprise, and she remembered they were supposed to be trying to make friends. "I mean, no, thank you."

For a second, all was silent. Then the dwarf pushed to his stubby feet with a dawning smile.

"Oh, sorry. I forgot."

The air around him shimmered, and the next second a lovely shape-shifter was standing in his place. Statuesque and serene, as if she'd been there the entire time. The princess let out a gasp of surprise as Tanya casually smoothed down her shirt.

"Why were you—" she started to ask, but Tanya flashed her an impatient look.

"Did you not hear me about the whiskey?" the shifter demanded. "How else was I supposed to get double rations?"

Katerina stared for a minute, then rolled her eyes and snatched up the wad of clothes. "I keep forgetting that my life is a circus now. I keep expecting things to be normal."

Tanya followed her up the hill into the trees with a broad grin. "Why in the world would you want things to be normal? They're so much more interesting as they are!"

The girls quickly finished dressing for the day and found a log overlooking the hectic little camp from which to eat their porridge. It was truly one of the most bizarre sights Katerina had ever seen. No matter which way she looked, there was a surreal sort of chaos.

Her eyes flickered from where Rose was entertaining a group of dwarves with a story about the night she'd lost her virginity (three times over), to where Craston was meticulously curling the tip of his beard, to where Dylan and Cassiel were quietly arguing, right over to where the tiny dwarf Tanya had been impersonating was furiously searching for his missing allotment of liquor.

Katerina took it all in with a secret smile, thrilled to be a part.

"Hey, thanks for going after Rose the other day," she said suddenly. Memories had been coming back to her in bits and pieces, but Tanya's defense of the poor shifter stood out clearly in her mind. "It wasn't her fault, and Dylan can be a little... overprotective."

"You think?" Tanya laughed and shook her head, picking at the lumps in the porridge. "It was nothing. To be honest, Cass was even worse. I thought he was actually going to take a swing at Dylan when you guys all got in last night."

"Take a swing at him?" Katerina repeated in bewilderment. "Why? What did Dylan do?"

"*You*, apparently." Tanya shrugged with a distinct lack of interest. "Or, at least, that's what Cassiel thought when he found you guys with the dwarves. He came back ranting and raging about how disappointed he was, how Dylan shouldn't have taken advantage—"

"But he didn't!" Katerina exclaimed. "He didn't do anything, *nothing* happened!"

"He knows that now. Dylan told him." Tanya chuckled softly at her panic, nudging her playfully in the side. "Relax, Kat. You're not the first girl to eat some magic berries, take off her clothes, and climb on top of a man. At some point along the line, it happens to all of us."

The obvious flaws in that statement aside, Katerina looked at her with sudden suspicion.

"How do you know that's what happened?" she demanded. "How do you even know what Dylan and Cass were fighting about? You weren't there."

"I was eavesdropping," Tanya replied without a hint of shame.

Eavesdropping. Of course, she was. Because, in addition to being able to impersonate anyone under the sun, the little troublemaker also had the uncanny ability to blend into the trees.

"Does Cass actually like that quality in you?" Katerina asked dryly. Unable to think of a word in her own defense, she settled for deflecting instead.

Tanya flashed her an angelic grin. "I don't see any reason why he has to know."

The princess shook her head, staring down into her porridge. "This day is going to be unbearable. I can feel it already."

Chapter 7

As it turned out, that sense of foreboding was a bit premature. Considering how gruff and brutish they could be, the dwarves turned out to be excellent traveling companions. They didn't stop very often—according to Craston, there was no higher benchmark for endurance than that of a dwarf—but when they did, they made a show of it. Barrels of mead, links of sausage, rind after rind of cheese emerged from deep in their knapsacks. Also according to Craston, there was no higher benchmark for hospitality than that of a dwarf so, although they had little to contribute themselves, Katerina and her friends shared in the spoils. For a group of teenagers who'd escaped the monastery with nothing more than a few daggers and a propensity for hunting rabbits, it was heaven on earth.

The dwarves themselves were an experience she'd never forget. Legs half the size of hers, and yet she found herself struggling to keep pace. Arms twice the width of her legs, and she soon found that there was no limit to what they could do. Halfway through the valley, she saw Craston courteously lift aside a fallen tree just so Rose and Tanya could walk through. Not long after that, he and two of his friends rolled a giant boulder into the river—claiming they didn't want to get their feet wet. Every mile was accompanied with rumbling laughter and song, and by the time the little company saw smoke stacks swirling over the rise of the next hill Katerina had borne witness to more bawdy jokes than one person could possibly handle. She had a brand-new vocabulary forming.

One she was sure her mother would have despised.

"Is that it?" She came to a stop beside Dylan, panting slightly to catch her breath as she stared over the ridged tree line. "The camp at Pora?"

The smoke spirals were too deliberate to be accidental. And too consistent to be mere campfires. They indicated a large group of people. Living intentionally off the grid.

"That's it." Dylan shaded his eyes and gazed out into the setting sun. They'd made better time getting there than even he had planned, but now that the moment was upon them he seemed strangely reluctant to take that final step. "I never thought I'd come back here," he whispered.

The princess glanced over in surprise, taken aback by his change in tone. There wasn't much in the world that made someone like Dylan hesitant, but here he was, openly dreading whatever was to come next. If she didn't know better she'd swear he was stalling.

"Why did you leave?" she asked quietly.

She was surprised it had never come up. From the bits of information she'd gleaned from the dwarves, combined with what she knew about Dylan's own past, the success of the rebellions and the demise of the Damaris bloodline meant the world to him. Born into a life of corruption and bloodshed, it was the only way he knew how to atone. She simply couldn't imagine him just walking away.

He didn't answer. Not right away. Instead, his eyes drifted over to Cassiel.

The fae was standing just a few yards away, also within the line of the trees. While the dwarves were cheerfully bustling around him, securing whatever final provisions were left before heading into the camp, he was frozen perfectly still. Gazing out towards the smoke with a truly indecipherable expression on his lovely face. There was anticipation there, but something else as well. Something that went far deeper. A profound kind of sadness that settled in his eyes.

A second later he felt them watching and snapped back to life, swinging his blade and satchel across his shoulder as if nothing had happened.

Dylan dropped his gaze with a sigh. "Serafina."

His voice was soft. Almost like a caress. One worn smooth by time. Katerina stared at him curiously, her eyes taking in every inch of his face.

"Who?"

He pulled himself back to the present and flashed a tight smile, lifting his own bag over his shoulders, along with her own. "Cassiel's sister. This is where she died."

THE GANG REACHED THE camp just as the sun was setting over the mountains, painting the valley with a brush of golden light. It illuminated the delicate leaves cascading down from the clustered magnolias, lighting up the coils of ivy wrapped around their base like magic ribbons. There was an evening breeze but, like everything else they'd come across in the valley, it was fragrant and warm, whispering through the white linen tents like they were tiny ships set sail on a grassy sea.

"It's beautiful," Katerina murmured, poised at the edge with the others, taking it all in.

Tanya nodded, while Rose gazed around with wide eyes. "It's... busy."

The shifter was right. When the princess had been told they were heading to a rebel camp, she had imagined just that. A rebel camp. Scores of men in dark leather, scowling around campfires and perpetually sharpening blades that never seemed sharp enough. A strong sense of the inevitable, offset with scraps of food and scattered supplies littering the ground.

But this? This looked more like a tiny village.

The first thing Katerina noticed were children. Lots of them. Just as many as there had been back at the monastery, maybe more. A little underfed, perhaps, but happy. Running about in huge, unsupervised packs, as they shrieked with laughter at their latest game. The next thing she noticed was the diversity. It seemed that hating the royal family was a universal pastime.

At first, there were all the usual suspects. Packs of burly men with roving eyes who had to be some kind of shifters. Little clusters of what Katerina had first thought were fireflies which, upon closer inspection, turned out to be pixies. Men and women with faces so pale and haunting, they could only be vampires. Goblins licking honey from an overturned jar. A group of fast-talking witches with herbs and little bones strung through their hair. If Katerina wasn't mistaken, she could have even sworn that she saw a neon-pink-haired fairy retching drunkenly into a bin.

But there were others as well. Others she had a harder time recognizing.

A girl with blue skin and sharpened fingers was absentmindedly pulling strips of wood off a nearby table, examining each one carefully before placing it into her mouth. A trio of men with fire for hair was laughing loudly over a game of cards. And a series of shadowy horses were lounging beneath the trees, their long manes dripping down their necks like tangled seaweed.

Katerina's eyes lingered with interest on the horses as a tall figure came up beside her.

"Kelpies," Cassiel said under his breath, following her gaze. "Don't go near them. They'll stay in that form just long enough to drag you to the nearest source of water, then they'll drown you with a laugh. They're strong, too. Surprisingly strong."

As he spoke, one of the horses looked over with an unmistakable wink.

Katerina stifled a shudder, making a mental note not to accept any rides. "How do you know that? Has that happened to you before?"

He dismissed the memory with an easy shrug. "I'm not so easy to kill."

It was said with that signature pretentiousness she'd come to expect, but the second the words were out of his mouth they took something with them. The haughty superiority was replaced with that same abstract sadness she'd seen earlier on the bluff. It tugged painfully at her own heart.

"Cass," she began, having no idea how she was going to finish the sentence.

But before she even could, Tanya walked forward and slipped her hand into his. He glanced down at her with surprise before the two headed off together, striding silently towards the biggest tent. They were replaced almost immediately by Dylan, who seemed to be scoping out the scene just the same as Katerina. His eyes took in every single detail as his arm wrapped around her shoulders.

"Are those ghouls?" she asked with a sudden whisper, staring in morbid fascination at a pair of genderless creatures in dark cloaks floating silently across the grass. They didn't seem to have eyes, but she could swear they were looking at her nonetheless.

"The rebellion doesn't discriminate in terms of membership," Dylan replied automatically, but as he followed her gaze an almost childlike shiver shook through his shoulders. "But stay away from them, too. Just from a psychological standpoint."

Katerina laughed nervously as the two of them grabbed Rose by the arm and followed along after Tanya and Cassiel. The dwarves had split apart almost immediately upon setting foot in the camp—promising to see them the next day at breakfast—and suddenly, the band of friends was quite on their own again.

They moved in a tight group, never allowing any one member to get physically separated from the rest. It was a casual strategy, but a deliberate one. One wrong step in this crowd, and you could find yourself on the wrong end of a blade or tentacle. And although Dylan had assured the princess that she would be perfectly safe despite her royal blood, Katerina wasn't so sure. Not that she doubted his intentions, but in this crowd she wasn't sure if anyone could be perfectly safe.

They came to a stop in front of a pair of thick wooden doors. Doors that were guarded by an even thicker pair of trolls. Katerina had to lift her chin just to see the top of them. Their hands flexed threateningly on the grips of their clubs, and for a split second the princess almost laughed.

Why do they need weapons? They can rip us apart with their bare hands. She was careful to keep that opinion to herself.

"Who are you?" The questions fired out like bullets, slightly slurred, as if the trolls were more accustomed to the classic 'point and grunt'. "Why are you here?"

Any sane person would have stuttered a hasty excuse and left. Any normal person would have fainted dead away. But Katerina's new friends weren't exactly normal. And she doubted they had ever been called sane. Dylan walked right up to the trolls, smiling like they were old friends.

"We're here to see Petra," he answered without fear. His hand didn't even twitch toward his blade, though he was well aware of Cassiel standing tall beside him.

The troll who had spoken squinted suspiciously. Or perhaps he was simply trying to unravel the words. They didn't seem very bright, trolls. But at that size, Katerina didn't see they had to be.

"Petra?"

Dylan tensed for a fraction of a second, but his smile never faltered. "Yes, is she here? She isn't expecting us," he added casually, "but if I remember Petra's moods, she'll be none too happy that her honored guests were left out in the cold."

The trolls straightened up immediately, staring down with wide saucer eyes. "*Honored* guests?"

Dylan stepped back at once, whilst Cassiel lifted his chin with that look of superior disdain that Katerina knew so well. "I happen to be a rather famous minstrel. I'm shocked you haven't heard of me."

Rose snorted under her breath, and Tanya stomped on her foot. The trolls, on the other hand, were completely taken in, staring at the fae with a look of almost cartoonish awe.

"...*famous?*"

"Yes," Cassiel answered shortly, looking down to examine his nails. "Now, if you don't mind, we're in a bit of a rush. If my vocal cords get cold... you don't want to hear what's going to happen." He shuddered dramatically and moved his hands gracefully. "Is Petra here, or shall we proceed to lodge elsewhere?"

The trolls shared a quick look then stepped back at the same time, pulling open the doors to allow the friends to pass through. They did so quickly, sticking close together and keeping their hands and eyes carefully to themselves.

It wasn't until they were safely inside that Katerina shot Cassiel a sideways look. "A minstrel?"

He returned the look with a very solemn stare. "Katerina, I happen to have a beautiful speaking voice. I'm sure you can only imagine it in song."

"Oh, I'll get right on that," she vowed sarcastically. "Imagining it."

The gang fell silent as they passed through the outer cloak room and headed into the main hall. It was far and away the largest building in the camp, a gathering place that seemed to double as the mess hall. Long tables stretched from one end of the other—most of them still laden down with plates of half-finished food—and every few feet or so there stood another tall pitcher of ale. Some of the food remained, Katerina noted. The ale was completely gone.

"This reminds me a little of my old village," Rose said quietly as they headed down the pathway in the middle, towards the shorter table facing them at the end. She cast Dylan a wistful glance. "What about you? Did your pack have a place like this?"

Katerina's heart skipped a beat as her eyes flew to his face. As far as she knew, she and Cassiel were the only people to know that Dylan had royal blood of his own. And, judging by past events, she'd guess he wanted to keep it that way.

Sure enough, he answered only with a quick smile. "Mine was a little different."

Yeah, as in twice the size and ten times the gold?

"But you're right," he continued suddenly, his blue eyes tightening with a distant nostalgia as he glanced around. "This place brings back a lot of memories..."

As soon as they reached the end of the long walkway, the five friends pulled up to a sudden stop. They were standing in front of a short table connecting the adjoining rows, like where the bride and groom would sit at a wedding. At first, Katerina couldn't see much over the ranger's tall shoulder. Then her eyes widened as a strange woman slowly got to her feet.

She was taller than any person the princess had ever seen. Towering over the imposing men standing beside her. She was so tall that Katerina thought she might not be exactly human. But she certainly looked human. With wide-set onyx eyes. High, angular cheekbones. Thin, pale lips. And a chin that narrowed down into a sharp point. Each feature looked like it had been cut dramatically into her face from chiseled stone. Something like marble. Cold and white and unyielding. It was a beautiful face. Terrifying, but beautiful at the same time.

Petra, she thought, instinctively straightening. *It couldn't be anyone else.*

When she saw them, the woman pushed gracefully to her feet. Her hair—pale blonde and densely braided—hung long past her waist, and her eyes seemed to dance with their own icy fire as they swept over each member of the young consortium in turn.

"Dylan. Cassiel." She said their names with great fondness and familiarity, but also with a hint of surprise. As if she'd never again expected to see them in her hall. There was also a ringing authority in every word, a commanding presence that could never soften away.

Both men stepped forward and Katerina bit back a smile. She wasn't the only one who'd straightened up. Something about this woman made you stand at attention. They bowed their heads at the same time before raising them to look her in the eyes.

"It has been a long time."

Her voice filled Katerina with a strange combination of dread and reassurance, lilting with an accent unfamiliar to her ears. The woman's age was also impossible to determine. If she had to guess, Katerina would say she was somewhere in her late forties. But, at the same time, she got the strangest impression that age wasn't really a factor to this woman. It was merely an afterthought.

"It certainly has," Dylan replied. "I wasn't entirely sure we'd still find you here."

"Where else would I be?" She made a wide gesture to the hall before returning her focus to her unexpected guests. "Although I'm surprised you were able to gain access so easily." Her eyes sparkled knowingly as they fell upon the fae. "What were you this time? A violinist?"

Cassiel shrugged stiffly, as if it wasn't that far out of the realm of possibility, while Dylan rolled his eyes with a grin. "You know trolls. Sometimes it's better to just confuse them. Otherwise, they're a 'smash now, ask questions later' kind of breed. You know this," he continued with a hint of caution. "I'm surprised you have them guarding the door."

"We haven't had visitors in quite some time," Petra answered briskly. "And those who come usually don't have the audacity to walk up to a pair of trolls. Not that audacity was ever your problem. Either one of you." Her eyes swept over both the ranger and the fae with the hint of a smile, and Katerina was suddenly reminded very strongly of Michael. "You had other problems."

"We still do," Dylan said quickly, getting to the reason for their visit. "I have a bit of a story to tell you, and I'm hoping you'll reserve judgement and have an open mind—"

"*Dylan*," Petra's voice tightened sharply, and Katerina was suddenly reminded of the tone a mother might use when censoring a wayward child, "what is this?"

It took a second for Katerina to realize the terrifying woman's eyes were locked on her. Just another second for the fear to kick in.

What is this. Not *who*. Katerina was just a bloodline to her. A wretched name and the very symbol of everything these people had gathered together to destroy.

The princess inched closer to Dylan, suddenly longing for the friendly faces of the trolls.

"This is Katerina Damaris," he answered quietly. Quiet—and yet, every single person still milling about the hall seemed to freeze and the same time. "She needs our help."

The hall was abandoned immediately, the remaining food was cleared away. In just a matter of seconds every single creature in the massive building had disappeared, leaving not a single buffer between the princess and this terrifying woman. Not a single witness to whatever was to come.

She won't kill me. Dylan said she won't kill me.

Katerina chanted it over and over in her head. But the more she did, the weaker it got. For one of the first times, her fearless leader didn't look quite so sure of himself. That signature confidence was gone and he was staring at Petra with worried, entreating eyes.

"Milady," he murmured, slipping into an old title of respect, "allow me to explain—"

"There's no need." She cut him off sharply, stepping slowly off the platform that elevated her table and walking their way. "You've already told me. Katerina Damaris needs my help."

She was even taller up close, standing a full head higher than both Dylan and Cassiel. A thick band of what looked like knotted wood held back her long hair, and when she got closer Katerina could see a spidery vein pulsing angrily by her eyes.

The next second, she was holding a sword. One she'd conjured out of thin air.

"Wait!" Dylan cried, yanking the princess backwards as he simultaneously threw his body into the weapon's path. "Just listen—"

"There is no need to wait, there is no need to listen." Each word was like a nail pounded into a coffin, sealing the wood forever shut. "You have brought a Damaris to my doorstep, Dylan Aires. You of all people should know what that means."

The blade swung quickly, but Dylan was quicker. He intercepted the edge with his own long dagger—the only weapon that had survived the exodus from the sanctuary. It looked comically small compared to the four-foot sword in her hand, and a second later she twitched the handle and sent his flying. The sword came up again, and for the second time he threw his body in its path.

"Petra—stop!" he pleaded. "You don't understand!"

Another pair of hands wrapped quickly around Katerina's shoulders. She wasn't sure if it was Tanya, Cassiel, Rose, or all three—but they pulled her swiftly away from the action. Dylan, on the other hand, stayed planted exactly where he was.

"You're seeing her only as a name, but there's more to her than that," he insisted, chest rising and falling rapidly as the woman with the sword came closer. "She came to me whilst fleeing from her brother. I *swear* to you, she isn't what you—"

Katerina let out a silent gasp as the tip of the sword flicked suddenly beneath his chin. He stopped talking at once, freezing perfectly still as the blade reached briefly under his shirt and came back a moment later with a delicate silver chain. Her mother's pendant gleamed at the end of it. Flashing fiery shades of crimson and gold as it glittered on the edge of the polished blade.

"Where did you get this?" Petra murmured in a strange voice. Her eyes were transfixed by the magic stone, staring as though she was remembering something from a dream. "The girl... she gave it to you?"

Dylan was panting softly, the tip of the sword still hovering an inch from his heart. "You can't kill her. You need to listen to me. She isn't what you think."

For the first time, his words seemed to hit home. Petra's eyes pulled abruptly away from the pendant, as if she'd been yanked out of a trance, before coming to rest on Katerina. They lingered there with such unnerving intensity it was as if they were burning into her very skin. A second later they softened just as quickly, the ice around the pupils replaced with a lighter kind of grey.

"No. It appears she is not."

The sword vanished and she lifted an ivory hand, beckoning the princess forward. Katerina swallowed hard and was about to comply, but Dylan didn't relax his position in the slightest. He was still angled protectively in front of her, silently refusing to move.

Petra's eyes swept over him with a maternal smile. "I will not harm her, child. You were wise to bring her to me."

He hesitated, still not entirely convinced (probably because he'd just recently avoided decapitation), then Katerina put a tentative hand on his arm and he relaxed by a hair, shifting aside to allow her to pass. To be perfectly honest, the princess didn't know why the hell she was moving forward. After seeing her unbeatable warrior freeze with the tip of a broadsword pressed against his chest, she should have been running the opposite direction.

But there was something about this woman that made her want to trust. Something about the way the pendant gleamed when it reflected in her eyes.

"Milady." She stopped nervously in front of the woman and resisted the urge to give an awkward curtsey. It was strange enough parroting Dylan's title of respect. Katerina didn't think *she'd* called another person 'milady' in her entire life. The title had always been applied to her. "I'm—"

"I know who you are, child." Petra reached out and took her by the hands, pulling her a step closer. "I saw only Damaris, but I should have seen it immediately. You have your mother's eyes."

My mother? Katerina froze, looking down at their hands. The woman's skin was much warmer than she'd been anticipating. She'd expected it to be ice-cold. "You knew her?" she asked suddenly, lifting her head. "You knew my mother?" She didn't know exactly what had made her ask the question. She certainly hadn't been planning on it. But, even as she said the words, she was suddenly sure they were true.

Petra stared at her quietly, that knowing fire dancing in her eyes.

"Her pendant," Katerina continued, cautiously staring back. "You've seen it before?"

This time the woman smiled. An open smile, one that seemed to peel decades of worry and strain off her chiseled brow. For a fleeting moment, Katerina felt herself transported back. To an older time, when the world was lighter. When the problems that had begun to overtake them had not yet come to be. When people could meet in the open. Walk in the light.

"Of course I've seen it," Petra answered warmly. "I'm the one who gave it to her."

Chapter 8

You'd think that after a revelation about someone's dead mother, the conversation would focus on that. Or the mentioned relic. Especially if that mother happened to be a queen. Especially if that queen happened to be gifted with a mysterious pendant that seemed to have a life of its own. Katerina didn't even know the pendant was special, aside from the fact that it had been her mother's.

But that wasn't the case. Petra refused to say more after dropping that bombshell. Despite Katerina's numerous objections, which were eventually silenced by Tanya's sharp poke in the ribs, it seemed their audience with Petra had ended. She wouldn't tell Katerina anything about the pendant, her mother, or answer any other questions Kat had.

The strange lady dismissed them into the night after bestowing upon each a welcoming embrace, lingering specifically upon those she already knew.

"Apologies for the sword." She kissed Dylan lightly on both cheeks, her eyes twinkling and bright. "Rest assured, I had no intention of skewering you alive."

Dylan shot her a rueful grin, finishing what seemed like a pre-rehearsed quote. "But anything can happen in the heat of the moment?"

"That's right."

She gave him a parting smile and turned to Cassiel. He alone hadn't moved during the little skirmish that had almost claimed two of their lives. It hardly seemed to register. And he alone had said not a single word to their hostess, despite having been directly addressed. To be honest, she was the first stranger they'd met with whom Cassiel wasn't unshakably polite.

Not that she seemed to mind. The sadness in her eyes reflected the sadness in his.

"There's a small memorial," she said quietly, "in the grove of jasmine beside the river. If you like, we can go there together..."

His eyes flashed and she fell suddenly silent. Even Katerina looked down at her shoes. Petra obviously didn't know him that well if she expected him to be coddled.

The woman sighed and gave his shoulder a gentle squeeze. "There's also a tavern at the end of the road."

Okay... maybe she knows him after all.

They were dismissed with instructions as to where they could spend the night. According to Petra, they would speak more in the morning. For now, she needed time to digest what had been said. The rest of the world might have been racing by, but the woman moved at her own pace.

With a reluctant word of farewell, they headed out of the main hall and back out into the night. It was darker now. The stars had come out and the trolls had apparently gone home, leaving the doorway unattended. The five of them paused for a moment, gazing out over the rebel camp.

Pora seemed to be the place where every displaced creature in the five kingdoms had ended up. Everything—from the orphaned children, to the magical refugees, right down to the packs of stray dogs—screamed the need for a better life. Not with their faces. On the surface, the rebels of Pora were a happy bunch. Laughing together as they walked through the streets. Perpetual smiles carved deep in the lines of their faces. With their resilience. That silent yet perpetual need to keep going. To keep themselves protected. To find a way to survive.

People shouldn't have to live like this, Katerina thought to herself, gazing across the courtyard to where a girl of no more than six or seven was hauling up water from a well. *They deserve better.*

"You okay?"

She glanced up swiftly as Dylan put his arm around her shoulders, hoping the sudden welling of emotion didn't show on her face. "Yeah—fine. It's just... been a long day."

He nodded understandingly. "Petra can be a little draining. But she means well. And there's no better ally to have on your side. Don't let the little incident with the sword fool you."

Katerina snorted under her breath. Only Dylan would describe the terrifying skirmish on the stone stairs as 'the little incident with the sword.' Like it was all a misunderstanding. Then her smile faded as she considered Petra once more. The woman was full of secrets. *Clearly, she knew my mother.* "What is she?" Kat asked quietly, gazing up into his eyes.

He frowned thoughtfully. "I don't exactly know. She definitely has some shifter blood. I'd be willing to bet she has some witch blood, too. Whatever she is—she's as old as these hills."

So, I was right. She's like the female counterpart to Michael.

"How are you doing? Are you all right?"

Katerina glanced over her shoulder to see Tanya speaking in a soft undertone to Cassiel. He had that same expression as when he'd looked down upon Pora from the trees, and in spite of what looked like great resistance his eyes kept drifting to the river. Toward his little sister's memorial.

Dylan followed his gaze, seemed to silently read his mind, then clapped him firmly upon the shoulder. "Shall we go and get a drink?"

The fae shook quickly out of his trance and tore his eyes away, latching on to the tavern at the end of the road like some kind of life raft. "*Drinks.* I may need a few. Or many."

With that, the five friends wound their way through the village and pushed open the door to the noisy bar. They were all the same, Katerina realized. From the tavern where she'd met Dylan, to the place where she fell into a ghost, right down to the one at Talsing Sanctuary. A bar was a bar.

After the day they'd had, it was a welcome relief.

"You guys get a booth," Dylan instructed. "I'll get the whiskey."

"Bring the bottle," Cassiel replied.

The four of them settled down in the far corner, while Dylan disappeared to the bar. They received their fair share of curious gazes and whispers, but by this point they were basically immune.

They were, however, abnormally focused upon each other.

"So... does anyone want to tell me what the hell is going on?"

The others looked up in surprise to where Rose sat in the middle, chewing distractedly on her lower lip as she waited for an answer. Cassiel pushed to his feet with a silent sigh.

"I'm going to help Dylan," he muttered, and walked away.

Rose stared after him with wide eyes, then returned a bit guiltily to the girls. "Did I... should I not have said anything? I didn't mean to pry, I just don't know what's going on. Nothing makes sense."

Sometimes Katerina felt sorry for the shifter. Yes, she had certainly pushed her way into the group by force, but they'd already started to accept her. It wasn't her fault that she hadn't been there from the beginning. That there were significant gaps that needed to be filled.

"Cassiel has five sisters," Tanya began softly, then instantly corrected herself. "*Had* five sisters. The Fae tend to have large families."

Katerina froze curiously on the bench beside Rose, listening intently. She'd only been told the basics. This was news to her, too.

"Sisters?" Rose lifted her eyebrows in surprise. "I can't imagine him with siblings. He seems like such a spoiled only child."

The princess laughed softly, thinking the same, while Tanya flashed a smile. "He was the only boy. That's probably what it is." Her smile faded as she whipped out a blade and began tracing patterns in the wood. "At any rate, he *had* five sisters. They were all killed in the uprising under Damaris rule." Her eyes flickered to Katerina. "The youngest was killed by your brother's dogs."

A sickening weight froze in the pit of Katerina's stomach. Like she'd swallowed an icy stone.

That must have been her. Serafina.

At this point, she didn't know what to say. She was so far beyond guilt, so far past unspeakable remorse, that it couldn't be put into words. Apologies fell short. *Everything* fell short.

Especially here. With these people. In this place.

"A bottle for the travelling minstrel, and another for us to share," Dylan announced, setting a handful of glasses upon the table as he took a seat beside Katerina. "With any luck, Cass, we'll get you to sing us a song or two before the night is done."

A good third of the fae's bottle was already gone. He'd apparently drained it on the walk back to the booth, and he seemed already in considerably better spirits. A faint flush appeared on his pale skin, followed by the hint of a grin. "Only if you dance. And only if it's actually *on* the bar."

"Done," Dylan replied without hesitation. He turned to Katerina with a smile. "So, what are you girls talking about? Me, I hope."

The trio of women shared a tense glance before Tanya flipped her hair over her shoulder with a casual grin. "We were actually just wondering how many of those unclaimed children running around outside were the two of yours. I swear one of them had pointy ears..."

For the next few hours the gang relaxed in yet another tavern, in yet another place, under the familiar soothing hands of alcohol. The two bottles Dylan had produced didn't turn out to be nearly enough, and by the time Craston and his dwarves joined them a little after midnight they were already a good six bottles in. That's when they really stepped it up.

As usual, Katerina did her best to keep pace, but she didn't have nearly the tolerance that the others did. Dwarves were natural-born drinkers, shifters had a supernatural resilience (although that was new to Katerina as well), and no matter what ungodly amount of liquor was consumed it hardly seemed to affect the fae. Four hours in they were just getting warmed up, while she was already laying her head discreetly upon the table.

"You ready to call it a night?" Dylan asked quietly, leaning down to whisper with amusement in her ear. "I can walk you back to where we're all sleeping."

"No," she blurted, bolting up quickly and blinking her eyes. "I'm awake. Not even tired."

His lips twitched as his eyes softened tenderly. "You're an adorable lightweight, have I ever told you that?"

"I am not," she replied defensively, pinching herself under the table just to stay awake. "You might have forgotten, my friend, but I'm a shifter, too. And a *dragon* at that. I can handle just as much as you. Probably more."

His eyes flickered automatically around the bar before returning to hers with an even wider grin. "Do you want to say *dragon* a little louder? I don't think the royal cavalry heard you."

Katerina ignored this, pushing shakily to her feet. "I'm going to get another bottle. Then we'll see who can liquor their handle." His head tilted curiously to the side, and she sensed she might have gotten that last part wrong. "Stand aside."

"Not a chance," he chuckled, pushing to his feet as well. "I'm going with you."

"Oh, relax." She shoved past him with a grin. "It's right over there. I'll be back in a second."

He looked like he was about to protest, when something Craston said caught his attention and he turned away. She took the opportunity to slip past him, stumbling clumsily through the swarm of supernatural creatures towards the bar.

Has it always been so warm in here, she wondered absentmindedly, leaning against the counter as she waited for the barman to return. *Has there always been two of everything?*

She tapped her palms rhythmically upon the sticky wood, completely oblivious to everything around her, until a seven-fingered hand waved suddenly in her face.

"Did you want to order something, honey?"

She looked up in surprise to see that the bartender had returned. All six arms and forty-two fingers of him. She wondered if it was an unspoken rule: people who owned a tavern had to be built with a little bit extra just to keep up with supply and demand.

"Yes," she said quickly, flashing an intoxicated smile. "I'm sitting with that big table over there and we're going to need another bottle. I'm just... not sure what it's called."

The dilemma hit her all at once and she glanced up uncertainly, her eyes sweeping the rows of bottles lining the shelf. A second later, she pointed in triumph. "It's the one with the clover."

The man paused, then gave her an amused smile. "You mean the Ace of *Clubs*? You ever played cards, princess?"

"No." She didn't know what that had to do with anything. "Anyway, it's got a purple top."

"Yeah," he chuckled to himself, "I know. That's empty for display purposes, but I think we've got another carton in the back."

She followed after him to an open-air hallway that let in the chilly night. In one direction was the bustling tavern. In another, an aged supply room, packed to the gills. She swayed gently on her feet, waiting patiently as he rifled through the crates, before something he'd said echoed suddenly through her mind.

"*Princess*." Drunk as she was, her face still managed to pale. "Why did you... I mean, I don't know what you've heard, but I—"

"Don't worry," he interrupted with a knowing smirk, "Petra already put out an order not to touch you. It seems as though you might be of some value to us."

Put out an order? How the heck did she do that? We've been here the whole time. I haven't seen an order. "Oh, well..." Katerina tried not to act as off-balance as she was. "I'd like to think I *am* rather valuable—"

The man snorted and pried off the lid of a crate. Inside were the purple-topped bottles the princess had been looking for. "Take however many you want. Pay up front when you're ready."

"Oh, perfect! Thanks." The princess sank to her knees as he went back to the tavern, rifling through the identical bottles as she pulled them carefully out of the straw. The door was wide open, letting in all the noise from the bar, and she didn't even notice she wasn't alone until there was a tap on her shoulder.

"Remember me?"

Katerina whirled around and pushed to her feet in a single motion, stumbling slightly as the backs of her legs smashed up against the crate. In front of her stood a group of four pale-faced men. Four pale-faced men she was horribly certain she'd seen before.

"It's you..." She tried to sound strong, but her head was spinning and her voice came out as a hoarse whisper. "From the other bar. You tried to..."

The memory shuddered down upon her, locking her knees and freezing her in place. It had been one of her first nights on her own, the night she went to a tavern and met Dylan for the first time. He hadn't been with her yet, but the vampires had certainly picked up on her trail. It hadn't helped that, at the time, she'd been unintentionally doused in a spattering of blood.

"Yes, but your friend stopped me." The vampire was in front of her the next instant, moving so fast that her eyes couldn't follow. A swish of her hair and there he was, looking exactly the same as she remembered. Beautiful, pale, and dangerous. "Of course, I didn't know you were a princess then." With a long-fingered hand he reached out and caught a lock of her crimson hair, twirling it gently between his fingers. "I've never tasted royal blood..."

Scream for Dylan. Use your fire. Smash a bottle over his head.

Each idea stumbled half-formed through her head, but the alcohol had made her slow, and no matter how many times it happened she could never quite get over the paralyzing terror of a stranger openly threatening her life. Her mouth opened, but no sound came out. Instead, she watched the other vampires circle in a crescent moon around her. Closing in for the kill.

"Wait."

Did she say it aloud, or simply whimper it in her head? Vampires were as deadly as they were fast; she knew this from experience. She might not have wandered very far, but her friends would still not be able to get to her in time if she screamed. Her only hope was to appeal to the vampires themselves, if that was even possible.

"Petra told the camp that I'm not to be harmed." Why couldn't she get a handle on this bloody shaking? It was a wonder the words even made it past her lips. "You can't—"

"We are not residents of Pora, and therefore will not abide by its rules," the vampire replied with that same self-assured calm. "We are merely passing through and will be gone long before the others find your body." His eyes glittered as he took another step forward, wrapping his cool hand around the back of her hair. "It's nothing personal, princess. If circumstances were different, we might actually turn out to be friends. But I carry a blood grudge against your friend, whom I'm assuming is somewhere nearby. An unpaid debt. And *that*, I simply cannot ignore..."

Katerina saw every fleck of crimson in his dark eyes as he leaned towards her. Saw every threaded eyelash as he tilted his head. Felt the impossible grip of his fingers holding her in a strange sort of caress as he opened his mouth and revealed a pair of razor-sharp fangs.

Her eyes snapped shut just as her legs gave way beneath her. A handsome face flashed through her mind and, as ironic as it seemed, her lips curved up with the trace of a smile. *Dylan*. At least he would be the last thing she saw as she fell back into the darkness.

Except, she never quite got there.

A pair of cool arms caught her just seconds before she could complete the fall. At the same time she suddenly registered that the door had opened again, flooding the room with a fresh rush of the frigid night air. There were sounds now, in the darkness. Sounds of muted collisions, sharp cracks and muffled groans, followed by a loud profanity in a language she didn't understand.

She opened first one eye, and then the other. But it wasn't Dylan's face she saw. The handsome face kneeling over her in the dark belonged to someone she'd never seen before. A face just as pale and beautiful as her attackers, only this one was looking down at her in concern.

"Are you all right?"

His voice was different, too. A gentle, musical cadence that filled her with a sense of inexplicable calm, just as it began to slowly dawn on her that she was *not* about to die.

For a split second she stared at him in a daze. Then she blurted out the first thing that popped into her head. "I just wanted the one in the purple bottle."

The world went black.

Chapter 9

Katerina woke up to a very different world than the one she'd fallen asleep in. Or passed out in. But hey, let's not be technical.

She was still on the ground, but instead of being pressed up against rigid floorboards she was lying on something soft and pliable. A bed perhaps? Or even something more basic. The way it folded and bent under her fingers reminded her more of grass. There was a chill in the air, but she wasn't cold. Someone had placed some sort of blanket on top of her. A heavy one. No matter how hard she tried to wiggle her toes and fingers, she was finding it hard to move. Her head was heavy and her mouth tasted like blood. She could tell that if she tried to open her eyes the world would spin away from her, so she didn't do that yet. She lay there and took in slow, deep breaths.

The sounds were different, too. Gone was the perpetual hum of raucous conversation coming from the bar, replaced instead with the whisper of the wind through a canopy of leaves. It was quite peaceful, actually. Punctuated every now and then with the unmistakable sound of flesh hitting flesh. The sound of quiet panting as someone struggled to breathe.

But the fight is over, isn't it? The vampires got scared away?

There was a soft cry, followed by the same profanity she'd heard before. One that sounded harsh, despite the gentle voice making it. A voice she'd recently heard for the first time.

Are you all right?

The words echoed back to her as the man's handsome face floated through her mind. At the same time, another cry of pain rang out in the stillness. A sick feeling of dread rose up in the princess' stomach and she slowly pried open her eyes.

Oh, shit...

Sure enough, there was her savior. Bruised and bleeding on the ground. Fending off multiple attacks, though he made little effort to fight back. Attacks that were raining down, swift and without mercy, from Katerina's circle of friends.

"I'm telling you," he panted, shielding his face as Rose's spiked boot slashed across his unguarded arm, "I didn't do it. It was the others. Wait for her to wake up, she'll tell you—"

"You'd just better hope she *does* wake up," Dylan growled, seizing him by the collar only to punch him squarely across the face. "Otherwise you'll see just how reasonable we can be."

The man gasped in pain, then spat a mouthful of blood in Dylan's face, his dark eyes glowing with vicious resentment. "I freakin' hate shifters."

"Then you picked a fight with the wrong crowd." Tanya kicked him in the ribs with a strength that was truly baffling, considering her petite size. "Because, as it happens, we shifters fucking hate vampires." Another kick, this one followed by a quiet moan. "Especially ones we catch trying to *feed on our friend*!"

At her ferocious words the first two fell back and Cassiel and Rose stepped forward, each eagerly contributing their own bit of excruciating pain. The man crumpled onto his back, dark hair spilling into his face, just as Katerina's sluggish brain woke up to the obvious realization.

Vampire. This man is a vampire.

The thought filled her with unspeakable terror, until the other part clicked slowly into place.

...but he saved me.

And then finally.

And the others are going to kill him, because they don't know.

"WAIT!" she screeched, pushing dizzily onto her elbows. The world tilted around her and she squeezed her eyes shut, still forcing words into the void. "It wasn't him! It was the others! He was the one—" she cut off with a gasp, trying to catch her breath, "he's the one who saved me!"

The group of friends went suddenly still. Their eyes fixed on the princess, then travelled slowly down to the broken vampire bleeding in their midst. A second later, Dylan flew away from the circle and slid to his knees beside Katerina, gathering her delicately into his arms.

"You're awake." He breathed the words more as an affirmation to himself than to anyone else listening, closing his eyes in unspeakable relief. "We thought it was just an awful concussion, but your pulse was so faint..."

Katerina nestled instinctively into his arms, taking silent comfort in the feel of his steady pulse beating against the back of her head. But even as she did so, something cold and wet leaked from his sleeves onto hers, and she looked down in horror to see they were stained with blood. "Dylan... that man..."

The ranger seemed to remember at the same time. His face paled as he glanced over his shoulder, staring with dawning horror at the vampire on the grass. Nothing the four of them had done was necessarily permanent, but it wasn't hard to see the guy was in bad shape.

There were giant tears in his skin, smearing his fair skin with a layer of blood, and judging by the delicate way he was holding himself they had broken several major bones. He lifted his head when he sensed them looking at him and drew in a painful breath. Those dark eyes bypassing Dylan completely as they came to rest on Katerina. They lingered there for a moment before his lips turned up in a humorless smile.

"Nice of you to finally wake up."

"WOULD YOU GIVE HIM some air? Stop crowding him!"

"You're the one who's waving that bandage, like, four inches away from his face."

"At least I'm trying to help him," the first voice snapped back. "Unlike you, who banged his broken leg on the doorframe when we made our way in here."

"That was an *accident*! How many times do I have to—"

"Could everyone just bloody leave me alone?" the vampire asked quietly.

There was something inherently frightening about him, but something strangely disarming as well. As if he was just a normal person who'd woken up one day to find he had the powers of the undead. The others fell instantly silent as he propped himself shakily against the headboard of the tiny bed, leaving a trail of smeared crimson in his wake.

"I don't need your help," he gritted against the pain, "I just need to feed. The blood will heal me."

There was a moment of silence, then Dylan answered as steadily as he could.

"We'll get you some blood, then." The color had yet to return to his face after realizing his grievous mistake, and although it was clearly torture to remain in such close proximity there was no way in hell he was letting the guy out of his sight. "Tanya, go down to the bar. Get as much as you can carry and bring it back here. Rose, go with her and help. Be as quick as you can."

Both women raced off to do as he asked, just as the vampire tried in vain to push to his feet. "That's not necessary. I can go myself." But even as he said the words one of his legs gave out beneath him, and he collapsed back on the bed with a tortured cry. "Freakin' shifters!"

Dylan and Cassiel shared a stricken glance before kneeling beside the bed once more with matching looks of atonement. As soon as the princess had woken up and cleared his name, the friends left the forest behind and swiftly relocated to their quarters within the camp. They were simple rooms; very similar to the ones they shared at the monastery. Basic furniture with only a few tapered candles to light the way. Candles that spilled dark shadows over across their faces as they gazed at the vampire in the dark.

"I'm so sorry," the fae said quietly, sincerity ringing from every word. "We'll do everything in our power to make it right. You have my word."

The vampire shot him a dark look; clearly the word of someone who'd spent the last half hour trying to kick in his ribcage wasn't worth much. Dylan leaned forward to try his luck.

"You have to understand how it looked," he continued softly. "By the time we got in there, the entire place was covered in blood. And you were kneeling in the middle of it, holding Kat—"

"—at which point you thought, 'just another despicable vampire,'" the guy interjected, his gentle voice growing unexpectedly cold. "Let's drag him into the woods and beat the crap out of him while we wait for our friend to wake up. Never mind the fact that she doesn't have a mark on her."

There was a lengthy silence, after which Dylan bowed his head with a look of deep remorse. "Yeah, we did that."

For few agonizing moments, the room was quiet. The vampire was pulling in ragged breaths on the bed, and Dylan and Cassiel looked about two seconds away from taking their own lives.

Neither of them offered him their blood, Katerina noticed. Desperate as the situation as, she didn't think it even crossed their minds. But the second she hobbled her way over from the chair in the corner, that's exactly what she did herself.

"Here," she held out a shaking wrist, still a bit unsteady on her feet, "drink something. At least until they get back with some more."

"*Katerina*," Dylan admonished, jerking her back while Cassiel made a strange hissing sound under his breath.

The vampire, however, was staring at her with wide eyes. "You don't know what you're saying. Please—just lie down and rest. They'll be back any minute."

"But he needs blood *now*," she insisted, yanking her arm away from him and offering it out once more. "What the heck is wrong with you guys? *You* did this. *You* need to fix it!" She didn't understand. What the heck were they waiting for? But neither man made any move to come closer. And the vampire didn't seem at all surprised.

Finally, after another painful moment of silence, Dylan muttered under his breath. "It's not that simple."

Katerina opened her mouth to argue, but she never got the chance.

He's right," the vampire said softly. "It's not that simple."

At that moment, the door opened as Rose and Tanya came rushing back in with the blood.

It was packaged in neat little bottles. If Katerina didn't know better, she'd think it was grape juice or wine. The vampire grabbed the nearest one and the others looked discreetly away as he ripped into it with his teeth. The princess, however, watched in morbid fascination as he drained first one bottle, then the next, and then the next.

Before her very eyes, the wounds on his body began to close. Stitching themselves together as if sewn by invisible thread. There was an almost inaudible crack as his bones began to do the same thing, but although Katerina flinched in sympathetic pain the vampire didn't seem to mind.

From the second the blood came into the room his entire person was absorbed with it. It overtook him completely, filling him with an almost contagious calm as it flooded through his system. Reanimating his ashen features. Replenishing what was lost.

By the time he was finished, he looked like a completely different person.

"And with that... I'll bid you all a goodnight."

The empty bottles clattered to the floor as he hopped off the bed and swept lightly to the door, acting as if nothing had ever happened. The others bowed their heads silently, but Katerina's mouth dropped open as she stared after him in total bewilderment. A second later her senses kicked in and she took off running down the hall, catching up with him at the bottom of the stairs.

"Hey, where are you going?"

Forgetting the fact that he was a vampire and she was afraid of vampires, she grabbed him by the sleeve. It was still wet with blood, although there wasn't a single mark left on his body.

His eyes widened ever so slightly as he looked down at her in surprise. Whether from the question or the casual contact, she wasn't sure. He seemed accustomed to neither.

"Uh... somewhere far away from your homicidal friends." He extracted his sleeve with a hint of amusement, as if he found the entire conversation very strange. "Surely you can't begrudge me that. Not after their little rage game in the woods."

He turned again but Katerina jumped in front of him, blocking his path.

Rage game—exactly! Broken bones! An attack in the supply room! Any of this ringing a bell?

"Wait! You can't just leave!" she cried breathlessly.

His eyes flickered across her face, curious but decided. A second later, he swept gracefully past her towards the door once more. "I think you'll find that I can."

"No, I mean... don't." She tried to take off after him, but the world tilted dizzily around her and she put a steadying hand against the wall. "Just wait a second. *Please.*"

It was the please that caught his attention. His entire body tensed, as if he hadn't heard the word in a long time. When he glanced over his shoulder, he looked distinctly wary but oddly vulnerable at the same time. Their eyes met and the princess walked carefully forward.

"I'm Katerina."

Time paused as he looked down at her extended hand. Then he hesitantly offered his own.

"Aidan."

The princess' face warmed with a smile as they shook. The most unlikely of meetings. Two opposite ends of the spectrum, coming together in a poorly-lit hall.

"Thank you... for what you did." She tried to infuse as much emotion into the words as possible. It wasn't even close to enough. "I'm so sorry for what happened after."

A faint shadow clouded across his face before it lightened with an unexpected smile. A fleeting smile, but a smile nonetheless. "You must get really tired of that."

Katerina shook her head, unaware that she was holding her breath. "What?"

He gazed intently into her eyes. "Apologizing for things that aren't your fault."

Katerina's lips parted as she stared up at him in shock.

It was the first time anyone had ever said that out loud, though she'd found herself trapped in the endless cycle since the moment she'd left the castle. Perpetually haunted by the trail of devastation left in her family's wake. Forever weighed down with the associated guilt.

It was her birthright. And her eternal curse.

"I haven't..." she began, then trailed off. "Someone should apologize."

A strange emotion swept across his face, and even though he was the one who had almost been beaten to death on her behalf his eyes softened with unmistakable pity.

"Someone already has."

The world quieted around them, and for a moment Katerina simply stared.

Aidan's eyes weren't anything like the other vampires she'd encountered, even though each one was supernaturally bonded to share certain traits. They were dark, yes, but they weren't flecked with that terrifying crimson. Instead, they were fringed with a ring of burnt gold—a lingering remnant of humanity that brightened the planes of his face in spite of his fair coloring.

In most other generalities, he was very much the same. Pale, smooth skin. Lean, muscular build. Inky black hair that fell in elegant waves to the tip of his chin. He was handsome, abnormally handsome. In a way that was meant to draw people closer. Luring them in for the kill.

It was a chilling sort of beauty, one that sent shivers over Katerina's skin. But it was the eyes that set him apart. There was something different about those eyes. A goodness and a clarity. One that made you want to hope. One that made it almost impossible to look away.

There was a sudden noise behind them as a door opened and Dylan walked out into the hall.

Aidan glanced up, breaking their connection, then turned on his heel and swept briskly outside. "Stay away from vampires, princess," he called over his shoulder. "We're monsters, haven't you heard?"

THAT REST OF THE NIGHT, Katerina couldn't sleep. It didn't matter that she'd spent the entire day hiking through the river valley. It didn't matter that she was emotionally drained from the attack at the tavern. It didn't even matter that she'd sustained a rather massive concussion. Every time she tried to close her eyes, they snapped back open. Staring at the ceiling. Unblinking and wide.

"Dylan... are you still awake?"

She knew he was. The man hadn't been able to let her out of his sight. Petra had been more than hospitable, offering each of the five friends their own room, but he'd quickly abandoned his in favor of her own. Pulling up a chair beside the tiny bed to watch over her. Silently counting each of her quiet breaths—ever vigilant—even in her sleep.

Of course, sleep wasn't exactly on the agenda.

"What do you think?" He tilted around so his face caught the moonlight streaming in from the window, illuminating his tired smile. "Bad dreams, princess?"

She didn't answer. She simply scooted all the way to the wall and patted the mattress beside her. It was a tight squeeze, the reason he'd pulled up a chair in the first place. But after a little bit of adjusting, they both managed to fit onto the tiny cot. Wrapped in each other's arms. Her head resting lightly in the hollow of his neck.

"What did you mean earlier?" she asked abruptly, eyes fixed on the ceiling. "When I wanted to give Aidan my blood? You said I didn't know what I was talking about. That it wasn't so simple."

"Who's Aidan?" Dylan asked without thinking. Then he caught Katerina's chiding glance and tensed. "Oh." He was silent for a moment, considering his reply. "Blood is everything to vampires. Absolutely everything. On a primal level. To give yours away... it isn't a casual offer. You forge a connection. A deep connection. And it isn't easily undone."

Katerina bit her lip, trying to understand. She remembered the way Aidan had ripped into the blood with his teeth. How the rest of the world had simply melted away. She remembered the vampire who had attacked her, the almost sensual caress as he slipped a hand behind her neck. "Is it... romantic?"

Dylan paused for a moment, then shook his head. "Not romantic necessarily, but intimate. It bonds you. In a way you can never undo."

That was the last either of them spoke for a while. Katerina's mind was spinning with a thousand unanswered questions. A thousand splintered thoughts and images that danced, half-formed, through her mind. She'd been through a lot in the last few months. A lot more than she ever thought was possible. But amidst all the chaos and uncertainty, one thing remained clear.

There were still things about this world she didn't know yet. Secrets still waiting to be told.

"Dylan?"

He'd gone so perfectly still she thought he must have fallen asleep. But the second she called his name, his soft voice echoed back in the dark.

"Yeah?"

She hesitated, unsure how to say it. Unsure whether or not she should say it. But after what Tanya had told her back in the bar, there was a part of her that had to know. "How did Serafina die?"

Dylan froze to sudden stone, as if he'd been struck by lightning, transformed into a reclining statue. His breath stopped and his muscles went dead still. The only indication he was still alive was the rapid beat of his heart, pounding against the walls of his chest.

Katerina held her breath, cradled in his rigid arms. It was quiet so long that she didn't think he was going to answer. When he finally did, it was like he was pulling the words from a place deep inside himself. A place he'd tried to permanently lock away.

"There was a raid." His voice cracked and he cleared his throat. "On a supply caravan that was heading east along the river. We'd been dug into the forest for months and the wagons were easy prey. Sparsely guarded yet increasingly disruptive to the royal effort to push forward."

Katerina remembered hearing her father talk about such raids, re-assuring his knights and councilmen at dinner. A petty nuisance, he'd called them. As the months went by, they stopped being so petty. Eventually, he stopped talking about them altogether.

"It was just a raid." Dylan's voice trailed off to a whisper. "We'd done it a thousand times."

For a split second, he was overcome with emotion. His chest shuddered and he momentarily lost the ability to speak. Then he took a deep breath and pushed past it.

"They knew we were coming. Someone inside our own camp had tipped them off. What we'd thought was a caravan delivering food and supplies turned out to be a regiment of the royal army's best trained soldiers. With a pair of hell hounds to sweeten the deal." His face darkened to sudden shadow, his eyes going cold and still. "It was over quick."

A rush of horror washed over Katerina as the room fell into sudden silence. Yes, she would imagine it didn't take long. A group of poorly-fed, inadequately-supplied rebels against the royal infantry at the height of its power? It wouldn't take long at all.

A distant memory of the men and women screaming at Talsing echoed suddenly through her mind, and for a moment she felt as though she was transported back in time. Watching a younger version of Dylan, Cassiel, and his beloved sister rush bravely into battle. Weapons gleaming in the sun. High with false expectations. Prepared for yet another easy kill.

In her mind's eye, she saw those expectations change. Saw the looks of horror transform their faces as a hundred bloodthirsty soldiers leapt out to meet them instead. Saw the hitch in their breathing and that split-second pause during which their entire world changed.

If she knew anything about the rebels, a change in the odds wouldn't have been enough to stop them. They would have thrown their bodies into the fray. Metal clashing against metal. Fierce cries as their weapons and armor spilled over with blood. Giving every last breath they had to defeat the forces that opposed them. The unholy army standing in their way.

It would not have been enough.

And the hounds...

"The raid," Dylan continued suddenly. "I was the one who suggested it."

The entire time Katerina had been playing over the situation he'd been playing it over, too. Reliving every frozen moment in his mind. Living and dying with each breath.

"The caravan was bigger than we'd expected, and Cassiel wanted to wait until we had more men. I didn't." His eyes glassed over, distant and remote. "When I went charging in, he and Sera went rushing after me. Just like they always did. Every time."

Just like that, the story was suddenly finished. Another piece of the puzzle slid quietly into place. Another heartbreaking chapter was laid to rest.

Katerina waited a long time before breaking the silence. She scarcely had the heart. "She must have really been something. Serafina."

There was a crack in the ice. A little thaw through which Dylan almost smiled.

"She was. You would have liked her."

Somehow, despite the instinctual jealousy that arose at the very mention of Dylan's fearless, extraordinary ex, Katerina didn't doubt it was true. Whoever he loved must surely have been worthy of that love. And any family of Cassiel's was to be forever cherished.

She sighed quietly before nestling deeper into his arms. "I think I'll try to get some sleep now."

There was some quiet adjusting on the bed as the two of them settled in beneath the covers, entwining their tired bodies in the patch of light let in by the moon.

"Sleep well, princess," Dylan murmured, kissing the top of her hair. "Dream of better things."

Katerina closed her eyes and slowly drifted off against him. Lulled into rest by the steady beating of his heart, by the even rise and fall of his chest. He held her close as his eyes fixed on the ceiling. Wide and unblinking. Seeing shadows and people that were no longer there.

He was still staring when the sun came up the next morning.

Chapter 10

When Katerina woke the next morning, she was shocked to discover the pounding in her head was gone. The mental fog had lifted. Her movements were sure and precise. If the concussion hadn't done her in she'd at least expected to be dealing with the world's worst hangover, but it appeared that the old saying was true. Shifters healed fast. And if yesterday's booze fest was any indication of future troubles, Katerina had tapped into those powers just in time.

Dylan was still lying exactly where she'd left him. Staring at the ceiling. Lost in thought. He startled a little when she rolled over, then flashed a quick smile the way he did when he was covering for something and his mind had clearly been somewhere else. "Good morning, beautiful." Even his voice sounded tired, as if he'd been screaming all night instead of lying quietly by her side. "Did you sleep all right?"

"Better than you." She looked him carefully up and down, making mental note of the dark circles under his eyes. "Bad dreams?"

They both knew better. But neither was particularly inclined to dwell.

He flashed a tight smile, then pushed stiffly to his feet, offering a hand to help her up as well. There was still a stain of Aidan's blood smeared across his knuckles, one they noticed at the same time. Dylan flushed and stuck it back in his pocket. Katerina got up by herself.

"So, what's on the agenda for today?" she asked, suddenly anxious to get a move on. Their time in the camp had been interesting, to say the least, and she was ready for the next step. "Go see Petra, make her spill her the guts about my mom, and then head to the next camp or wherever?" Part of her wanted to ask him to take her to a field and let her practice shifting. Another part of her was terrified it might never happen again. Or maybe she was too scared to try.

Dylan crossed the room with a little smile, placing a steady hand on her scrambling fingers as they hastened to clasp her belt. She was still dressed in whatever the dwarf Wallington had graciously offered to spare, and the darn things seemed determined to slide right off. "Slow down there, turbo. How about breakfast, then we find you some actual clothes, *then* we go see Petra. You need to eat, Kat. You're skin and bones."

She ignored this, sweeping her hair back into a long ponytail. In the time since she'd left the castle, her morning routine had been drastically reduced. Forget crystal vials of powder and slender glasses of champagne, she was lucky if one shoe happened to match the other. "I'm fine," she said dismissively, "and we need to keep moving. You heard what Craston said last night, about the scouts seeing tracks out in the woods. There's no telling where they are, or when they might—"

"*Breakfast,*" Dylan repeated firmly, grabbing her shoulders to stop the perpetual forward momentum. "Then clothes. Then Petra. I'm responsible for your safety, princess. And right now, you're at greater risk from malnutrition than you are from any royal army."

Her initial bubble of energy popped at the inescapable logic in his words, and her shoulders wilted with a quiet sigh. Truth be told, she couldn't remember the last time she'd eaten something. "Fine. You're right. As usual." With a tired smile she reached up to take his hands, lacing her fingers through his own. "Does it ever get boring—being the responsible one?" She traced the lines of his palm with a grin. "Because if you ever wanted a break, I'd be perfectly willing to just..." Then she noticed the blood again. Her stomach clenched and her voice trailed away. "Dylan... your hand..."

His tender smile melted into a look of surprise as he glanced down, then faded entirely as he retracted his arm with a sudden flush. Without another word he walked to the pitcher of water on her nightstand, pouring a stream over his knuckles and quickly wiping the skin clean.

She watched him silently. A nervous question hovering on the tip of her tongue. "Do you think maybe we should find him?" she asked quietly, hesitant to stir the pot but crippled by guilt at the same time. "Tell him we're sorry? Make sure he's okay?"

She'd expected an automatic affirmative. Truth be told, she half-expected Dylan to say he'd gone out and done it last night. But it wasn't meant to be.

"He knows we're sorry," the ranger replied curtly, shaking out his long cloak before securing it briskly over his arms. "We don't need to find him again."

Katerina took a step back, stung by the harshness in his words. A complete stranger had swept in and saved her life, then suffered brutally for it at the hands of those who cared for her the most. As a result, his own life was almost taken. Didn't that warrant some kind of follow-up?

"I don't understand." She said each word slowly, trying to reconcile the facts. "You almost beat the man to *death*. The least you could do is buy him some breakfast—"

"He's not a man," Dylan interrupted suddenly. "He's a vampire."

Excuse me?

This coming from a man who'd accepted Tanya's strange lineage without batting an eye. A man whose entire life was built upon the concept of equality, the complete lack of discrimination.

It's no big deal that we almost killed him... because he's a vampire?!

Her shock must have shown on her face, because Dylan took one look at her then sat her down on the edge of the bed. He took a seat beside her, raking his hands through his dark hair.

"I know how it must sound, especially to someone who didn't grow up around such things, but the stereotypes around vampires are there for a reason. Most all of them are true."

Katerina didn't know what bothered her more. The words he was saying, or the fact that he so earnestly believed them. If the rest of her friends were any indication, he certainly wasn't alone. "But he's still a *person*," she insisted. "And isn't it you who lives his life by the mantra that every living creature deserves a—"

"They're not *living* creatures."

His premise, simple as it was, stopped Katerina right in her tracks. It wasn't that she was particularly surprised. She hadn't thought the term 'undead' was somehow metaphorical. But, strange as it might sound, she just hadn't thought that distinction mattered until now.

"But you knew that ghost in the bar," she ventured tentatively, glancing down at his hand. It might have been washed clean, but she could swear she still saw the blood.

"Ghosts were alive once; they're just spirits of people who haven't passed on. Vampires are the way they are. They can only destroy, never create. Existing only to feed off the life-force of others. It's made them callous, cold. Incapable of basic emotion. Some say they don't have a soul."

Don't have a soul? Was THAT metaphorical?

"Okay," Katerina held up her hands, determined to add a dose of practicality before the conversation strayed too far, "how could anyone possibly *know* that—"

"Believe what you like," Dylan said indifferently, pushing to his feet. "But never once have I met a vampire who meant me anything more than harm. They can't help it. The very essence of their nature demands the extinction of ours. A life for a life. Blood for blood."

There was something very final about the way he said the words, and Katerina let the subject drop. She remembered him saying something very similar on the night they'd first met, when he'd casually explained why there was a good chance the succubus barmaid wanted to kill him. He hadn't seemed to carry a grudge. But perhaps vampires were a different story.

"At any rate, we should head out." Dylan slipped his blade into its sheath and offered his arm with a handsome smile. "See if we can scrounge you up some clothes and breakfast."

Katerina pushed the discordant thoughts from her mind and wound her arm automatically through his. As many times as it had happened before, she was still getting used to it: falling asleep next to a beautiful man and waking up beside him the next morning. There probably should have been some kind of adjustment period. An embarrassing in between phase that she spent crippled in self-doubt. But it simply hadn't happened. Being with Dylan felt as natural as if they'd been together their entire lives. Like she was coming back to him... instead of finding him for the first time.

THE CHAMBERS WHERE Petra had placed them were on the cramped upper story of a rundown wooden shack. Perhaps it had been a building at some point, a local laundry service or merchant's shop, but it had long since fallen into disrepair. Katerina glanced nervously at the wooden floorboards, creaking and sagging with every step, before hurrying down the rickety stairs.

The others were already waiting on the main road. Dressed, armed, and in generally good spirits. The only problem was that there were only two, instead of three.

"What's going on?" Dylan asked as soon as they came within earshot. "Where's Rose?"

Cassiel shot him a long-suffering look, jerking his head towards the gorgeous little shape-shifter bouncing around beside him. "This one's too wired to eat, and Rose never made it in last night. She went off with one of the shifters we met back at the bar."

Nothing like almost slaughtering an innocent vampire to get you in the mood.

As if on cue, a door flew open from the adjacent building and Rose strolled leisurely out into the sun. Her clothes were disheveled, her hair was a mess, and her puffy lips were curved up with a rather self-satisfied smirk. Behind her, not one but two different shifters leaned wistfully in the doorway, staring after her with dreamy eyes.

"Well, good morning!" she called, stretching up her arms with a wide grin. "I hope everyone slept okay. I certainly didn't—*sleep* that is." She elbowed Katerina in the ribs, unable to resist throwing in a salacious wink. "I mean because of all the se—"

"Yeah, I got it. Thanks." Katerina shook her head, unable to resist a grin of her own. As the two had been talking, a third shifter had appeared in the upstairs window. He looked as dumbstruck as all the rest. "Think you've worked up an appetite? The guys are insisting that we—"

"No, screw breakfast. We've got to get moving." She rifled around in her bag, extracting a bundle of wadded-up clothes. "On that note, I picked these up for you last night. Consider it a belated payment for that dragon ride. Dragon... flight?" Her face screwed up thoughtfully. "What should we call it when we travel by dragon?"

Dylan rubbed his temples, looking very tired. "*Stop* saying dragon."

"You could call it 'your friend Katerina saving your derrière,'" the princess replied, but she took the clothes with a grateful smile. "So, can we go then? Back to see Petra?"

The others may not have understood the exquisite agony of being forced to wait for information on one's dead mother, but Katerina had been able to think of little else. And that was in spite of being attacked by a squad of vampires last night and saved by another.

And on that note...

"You know, I'm a little surprised at you." She shot Dylan a sideways glance as the five of them headed off to the main hall. "Mr. Swoops-into-save-the-day. Not only did you miss your big chance last night and *then* beat up the wrong guy, but you totally let the others get away."

Granted, he hadn't known he was letting her attackers escape until well after he and the others had almost exsanguinated Aidan. But still. There were standards to uphold. And male pride.

"I didn't let the others get away." He lifted his voice and called, "Cass?"

The fae glanced over his shoulder, met the ranger's gaze, then doubled suddenly back and pressed a handful of what looked like tiny stones into Dylan's hand. Jagged pieces of ivory, tipped with a dull scarlet stain. It took a second for Katerina to realize they were fangs.

"Seven hells," she whispered. "Please tell me those aren't..."

The two men shared a communicative look, then Dylan bowed his head in silent gratitude. A second later, he would his arm back around Katerina's waist as if nothing had happened. "Like I said, I didn't let the others get away." He kissed the side of her head, then pocketed the teeth with a cheerful smile. "I delegated."

BY THE TIME THEY GOT back to the main hall, Katerina's head was spinning. Whether it was a delayed reaction from the concussion or the fact that Cassiel had performed some gruesome late-night dentistry, she didn't know. Maybe she should have eaten breakfast after all.

Petra was sitting in the exact same place she'd been when they left her. Her long arms dangling over the chair like it was some kind of throne. In a strange way, she looked like some of the generals in the king's old war room. Not in appearance, of course. It was the look in her eyes. A look that put Katerina instinctively on guard. A look that made her wonder if, when the rebellion was over, the woman might want to keep that throne for herself.

"Children!" She threw open her arms the second she saw them, her eyes twinkling with a knowing smile. "I trust you all slept well."

None of them answered. Instead, five pairs of eyes shot to the floor. Katerina had the sneaking suspicion not much went on in Pora that the rebel commander didn't know about. She was willing to bet the others thought so, too.

"We were wondering if you'd come to a decision," Dylan answered evasively, cutting past the customary chit-chat and getting to the point. "About whether to support Katerina's claim."

There was a long pause, during which Petra deliberately slowed the pace of the conversation.

"You think I should support it?" she finally replied, her dark eyes drilling not into Dylan but into Katerina instead. "You think the Damaris bloodline has earned a second chance?"

Yes, say yes. A cautionary voice spoke up immediately in the princess' mind. *Tell her you couldn't be more different from your brother. Tell her you don't want to subjugate anyone, but only wish for peace—*

"No," Katerina replied quietly. "I think the Damaris bloodline long ago forfeited any right it had to a second chance. I think the wisest course of action is to exterminate the entire dynasty."

There was a sharp intake of breath as the others froze beside her. Dylan grabbed his blade. Petra cocked her head with sudden interest. That cautionary voice disowned her and left for good.

"But I thought the whole reason for this camp was *not* to judge a person based on their blood," the princess continued boldly, stepping forward away from the group. "It's the fundamental premise that binds you all together. To judge based upon merit and character, rather than whatever supernatural hand biology might have dealt. I thought you believe in equality, inclusivity. That those differences are what make us stronger. That they should be embraced."

A sudden sense of calm swept through her. A cool assuredness that steadied her voice and lifted her chin. She was a Damaris, after all. Those things had been entrusted to her to protect.

"On that... we both agree."

Her voice rang out over the long chamber. Filling every corner and drawing every eye as people from all breeds and backgrounds turned around to watch.

"I am a Damaris, that's true." Katerina planted both feet firmly upon the floor, keeping her eyes locked on Petra. "Born of the same bloodline. Rightful heir to a dynasty that's done terrible things. Destroyed countless lives. Brought about evils for which I can never hope to atone..."

A sudden hush swept over the crowd as the princess stood up to her full height.

"But I can certainly try."

There was a moment of silence, followed by a literal explosion of noise. Katerina hadn't realized how many people had crammed themselves inside to hear her little speech. Almost the entire rebel camp was pressed into the hall behind her. Upon hearing her words, a hundred people spoke up at once. Calling out in her favor. Calling out in support. Lifting their fists to the sky and pounding their feet until the very foundations of the building began to shake.

Katerina kept her eyes locked on Petra. The one voice that mattered. The only opinion to make any sort of difference. The woman stared at her for an endless moment, then bowed her head.

"In that case we will fight for you," she said simply. "When you're ready, when you've gathered the numbers you need—we will fight."

The princess' entire body exhaled with breathless relief. Behind her, the people cheered and screamed. Her friends crossed themselves, thrilled they weren't going to be burned at the stake.

And just like that Katerina Damaris started building her army.

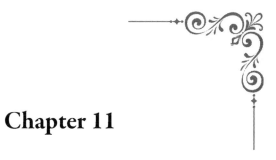

Chapter 11

The plan was simple.

Katerina and her friends would travel from camp to camp. Making the same pitch. The same passionate plea for resistance. Trying to get as many on board as they could. It helped a great deal that most of the camps in question seemed to take their lead from Pora. Formidable as she was, Petra was a renowned leader and her pledge of support was sure to bring about others.

When the time was right, and the last camp was secure, they would send word and the united rebellion would march as one against the castle. A princess at their helm. A dragon by their side.

Yes, Katerina had confessed to her shifter blood. Given the circumstances, she didn't see that she had much of a choice.

"I suppose you have many questions for me."

Katerina looked up in surprise to see Petra standing just over her shoulder. They had been strategizing, planning, for the better part of the morning, and the rest of them had taken a break to get lunch. She'd been just about to follow, when the commander caught her eye.

"Yes, I do." Suddenly, the hunger vanished. All Katerina could think of was her mother. "How did you know her?" she asked tentatively. That newly-found confidence vanished as well, and she was abruptly shy. "My mother."

"I didn't know her," Petra replied calmly. "I met her only once. It was shortly after her wedding, but already things were troubled. Already, they had started to unravel."

Katerina listened with bated breath, unaware that the others had left and the two of them were alone in the deserted hall. All her life, she had fought for information on her mother. All her life, she'd run into polite aversions and closed doors. How was it that *now*, halfway around the world, a stranger was giving her the answers she'd so longed to find? "What do you mean *unravel*?"

Petra opened her mouth to answer, then tilted her head to the side with a smile. "You just came from Talsing Sanctuary. Don't you already know, child?"

The journals. She must be talking about Michael's journals.

"My mother's secret, her power..." Katerina trailed off suddenly, gazing up at Petra with a trace of fear. "She told you what it was?"

For the second time, Petra smiled. But this wasn't like the first. A polite prompting, a little conversational nudge. This smile was pure warmth. Brightening the room and everything else in it. "She didn't have to. I'm a great deal older than I look, Katerina. It wasn't the first time I'd met a shifter in trouble. I'd seen magic like hers before."

So, she knows my mother was a shifter. And that must mean...

"Is that why you agreed to help me?" Katerina asked quietly. "You know your cause is my own, because I'm a part of the supernatural community as well?"

"Absolutely not!" Petra laughed sharply, sinking down onto one of the tables. "You think great evil cannot be done by shifters? For all we know, your twin brother was gifted with the magic as well. No, that's not why I agreed to help you. We are not defined by that magic alone." Her eyes were now a slate grey, as cold as a winter storm. "I agreed to help because of what you said. Because in that moment, you revealed who you are, Katerina Damaris. Someone worthy of the crown."

The princess could have imagined no greater compliment. And to have received it from such a person, in such a place... Her face flushed, and she bowed her head. But she lifted it just a second later, another question rising to the tip of her tongue.

"So, did you tell her that you knew? Why did you give her the pendant?"

Petra pushed slowly to her feet, ascending the platform stairs once more as the door opened at the far end of the hall. "I didn't tell her. A shifter's secret is theirs to keep. I would not impose unless specifically asked. But the poor woman had no one around to help her. For all intents and purposes, she was living in the belly of the beast. I decided to help in what small way I could."

"The pendant," Katerina finished, her eyes alight with wonder. "That's why you gave it to her? To help with her magic?"

Petra made a strange gesture. Something close to a shrug. "She needed a light to guide her way."

Thanks, riddle-master. But I was looking for something a little more concrete.

"But what *is* it?" Katerina asked, practically bursting with curiosity. Behind her, the hall was beginning to fill once more as those people who'd left to get food drifted back inside. "What does it do?"

She remembered the way it had dulled when she left the castle. The way it had glowed warm when her brother's hounds looked the other way. The way it burned Dylan's chest when they kissed.

"Hey."

Speak of the devil, and he will appear.

Katerina jumped in surprise as Dylan came up behind her, Cassiel, Rose, and Tanya right on his heels. For the first time in her life, she wasn't at all happy to see him. In fact, she rather wished the lot of them would just go away.

"I saw you guys were talking, so I just grabbed you something from the pub." He thrust a sandwich into her hands, looking curiously between her and Petra. "Is everything okay? You look a little... pale."

Pale. That was probably putting it gently.

Katerina whirled back around to Petra, feeling like she was about to explode, but the woman shook her head—a mischievous twinkle in her eyes. "Some questions are best answered in their own time, Katerina. And sometimes those answers are hidden right where you least expect."

It's official. She and Michael went to some summer camp together. The kind where they grew too tall, learned to change into weird animals, and were taught never to answer a question.

"Uh... thanks."

Petra laughed as the princess turned the sandwich miserably over in her hands, wondering what would happen if she simply commanded the woman to tell her.

Probably nothing. Or she might whip out that sword.

"So, does that conclude our business here?" Cassiel asked abruptly, glancing to the door. He had diligently sat through every minute of the strategy session. However, spending even a second of extra time in the rebel camp where his sister had died was clearly not something he was willing to do.

Petra's eyes softened and she nodded, sinking back onto her throne-like chair with an ingrained sort of dignity. "Yes, our business has reached an end."

"Excellent." Dylan's face lit up with excitement as his eyes drifted automatically towards the open road. The man may have had a slightly higher tolerance for the camp than his friend, but he wasn't built to stay in one place. That restlessness was deep in his blood. He was built for action. "In that case, we'll head straight on to Rorque. With any luck, the five of us can get there by—"

"I'm sorry," Petra interrupted smoothly, "but it's the six of you."

The rest of them paused, Dylan looking up in surprise. "Six?"

"Yes," the commander continued with a smile. "I have agreed to pledge my forces, and you go forth with my blessing. But you will do so with an emissary of my choosing. To represent Pora in all future discussions and act as my proxy whilst I remain here."

It wasn't an unreasonable demand, but the princess didn't relish the idea of adding someone new to their group. They'd only recently gotten used to the idea of Rose—throwing in a stranger so late in the game might prove disastrous to mission.

Of course, Katerina had no idea who this emissary was. Disastrous was putting it lightly.

A door adjacent to the head table pushed open, and a handsome man slipped inside. He moved with a slinky sort of grace, like a shadowy cat, and made not a single noise as he approached.

Oh, crap... Aidan. She stepped back, her stomach sinking into her shoes. Behind her there was a sharp intake of breath as the others closed their eyes in a shared grimace, cursing their unlucky stars.

The vampire looked surprised to have been summoned, but walked purposely up to Petra, settling in the chair by her side as if it was something he'd done many times before. He looked neither perturbed nor distraught to see the five friends, rather indifferent to their presence.

Of course, all that was about to change in a hurry.

Petra whispered something in his ear, and his face went pale. Even paler than it had been before. A bone-white. His entire body tensed, and for a moment that serene façade cracked.

"Wait... *what?*"

His eyes flashed to the gang before he lowered his voice and muttered something in a language Katerina didn't understand. When Petra did nothing but smile he tried again, more urgently this time, his handsome face rigid with defiance. This time, she actually laughed at whatever he said before leaning back in her chair with unmistakable amusement.

"It seems the six of you have already met." The gang stiffened and Aidan shot her a pleading look, but the woman had made up her mind. "Good. Then you'll have plenty to talk about."

No matter where they went, it was like the five friends couldn't catch a break. They wilted with simultaneous sighs, then tensed at the same time. Sitting at the table across from them Aidan leaned back in his chair and closed his eyes, muttering something that sounded strangely familiar.

"...*freakin'* shifters."

"*Now* do you wish we'd bought him breakfast?"

The five friends—and one angry vampire—had set off from Pora not long after receiving their sardonic marching orders. The sky was clear, and according to Dylan they could reach the next rebel camp with only a day and a half's walk. But that did nothing to lighten the mood. Hardly a word was spoken as the six of them made their way out of the river valley and up into the winding hills. Just the occasional, 'what are we supposed to feed him, anyway' or 'it smells like wet dog.'

Only Katerina had been able to find the levity in the situation. More than that, she found herself quite thrilled. Now, not only would she be able to properly thank the man who saved her from becoming a supply room horror story, but she could watch Dylan suffer to boot. Win-win!

"Breakfast?" the ranger repeated, lifting his eyebrows with a sarcastic glare. "Seeing as he'd probably like to have *you* for breakfast—no, I don't." There was a soft chuckling from up ahead, and he was seized with the sudden suspicion the vampire could hear them just fine. "Just... stay close to me, all right? No going off on your own."

Katerina quickly translated 'no going off on your own' as 'no going off with Aidan,' and rolled her eyes with an exasperated grin.

How could they not see it? The fact that they were the only ones playing at this war. Aside from the occasional 'wet dog' comment as he passed by the wolves, Aidan had been the model of manners. He was hand-picked by Petra. The camp's sole emissary. Had fought off his own kind just to save her life. How could they still be treating him as a threat?

Maybe because they know more about this than you do.

A quiet voice in the back of her head warned for caution, but Katerina ignored it as she skipped ahead to walk by Aidan's side. She also ignored Dylan's murderous glare, but at this point his self-righteous 'plight' was only going to make her giggle.

"So," she began with forced cheer, casting a sideways glance at the tall man walking beside her, "how did a vampire become the sole representative of the rebel camps?"

The second the words were out of her mouth, she regretted them.

You, she thought furiously, *why didn't I just say you? Why did I have to say vampire?*

Aidan gave her a quick look, but if he was offended he didn't let on. If anything, her flush of guilt seemed to amuse him. He tossed back his dark hair with a shrug, gazing up at the sunny sky. "Oh, you know... I ate all the other contenders." There was a hitch in her step, and he laughed quietly. "Just kidding. We vampires are known for our unparalleled sense of humor."

"Is that right?" Dylan called from a few yards behind, clearly displeased with the gory direction the conversation had taken. "You're known for your humor, huh?"

He and Aidan locked eyes for a split second before the vampire turned back to the princess with an unconcerned smile. "We also have unbelievably good hearing."

She stifled a grin. He'd clearly heard everything the others had been saying about him, not that they particularly bothered to lower their voices, but he just as clearly didn't care. Katerina didn't know if he was just impossibly hard to offend, or if he'd simply been offended so many times it no longer seemed to register. Either way, it was oddly endearing.

"So, do you know people in this other camp?" she asked curiously, trying to ignore the way Cassiel was just a step behind, his hand resting casually on his blade. "Have you been there?"

Aidan nodded, also ignoring the fae. "I know a few. If I'd known where you were planning to go, I would have sent word. As it stands, I'd be happy to go on ahead and prepare for—"

"That won't be necessary," Dylan said swiftly, wrapping his hand around Katerina's wrist as the entire party came to a sudden stop. "We actually have something to take care of before Rorque."

"We do?" Katerina asked in a low undertone as he yanked her closer.

The vampire looked similarly confused. "You told Petra we were headed straight there." It might take a lot to frighten one of his kind but disobeying the orders of the rebel commander was apparently quite high on the list. "She won't be pleased with an unscheduled detour—"

"Then she won't be pleased," Dylan answered evenly. "At any rate," he turned back to Katerina, "this isn't much of a detour. We just need to make a call..."

Without further ado, he fished around in his pocket and pulled out a tiny purple stone. For a second the princess just stood there with a blank stare, then her eyes lightened in astonishment. The seeing stone. She thought she'd lost it back at Talsing, but he'd saved it.

"How do you possibly have this?" she exclaimed, realizing just then that she'd given up on the thing for good. "I thought by now it was at the bottom of a cliff—"

Dylan shook his head, pleased to have surprised her. "It fell out of your pocket during training. I was going to give it back to you, but then... other things came up."

Yeah, like I turned into a dragon and burned the royal army to the ground?

The two shared a grin as the others chuckled quietly at the thought. The only one not laughing was Aidan. He was staring at Dylan's hand with a very peculiar look on his face. A second later, Katerina realized why.

Either by accident or by cruel intention, Dylan had fished out the severed vampire fangs along with the stone. They were scattered around his palm, like tiny macabre gravestones, each one representing a stolen life.

Oh, come on... was that really necessary?

Aidan froze perfectly still the second he saw them, his lips parting in surprise. A second later, he felt the eyes of the group upon him and quickly averted his gaze. Just a second after that, those feelings were buried down deep and he was back in control.

"A seeing stone?" he asked with forced calm. "Like the ones used by witches?"

Katerina nodded swiftly, trying to catch his eye. "It was given to me by a witch we met on the road. I've used it once already to contact a friend of mine back at the castle. I'm assuming that's what you'd like me to do again."

Her eyes flickered questioningly to Dylan, and he nodded.

"Before we go gallivanting around the countryside, trying to unite the rebel camps, I want to know how he's coming along on this dark wizard search. The last thing we want when we're travelling out in the open is another surprise..."

"*Another* surprise?" Aidan interrupted sharply. He'd made it a point thus far to accompany them as a mere observer, but this was too controversial to sit on the sidelines. "What kind of surprises have you five been having? And what do you mean 'dark wizard search?' There's a wizard after you?" Another fact they'd conveniently forgotten to mention to Petra. "And who exactly is this friend of yours that he's dabbling in the dark arts?"

"Wouldn't you like to know," Rose mumbled, but Katerina quickly cut her off.

"He's not dabbling," she explained hastily. "He's tracking. At least—that's what I'm assuming he's been doing. We've only gotten to speak once since I left the castle, and that was before we went to Talsing. He's a wizard—my friend. His name's Alwyn."

"I know who Alwyn is," Aidan interrupted with a bit of a frown. "He's been a fixture at the castle a great deal longer than you. I just... didn't know he was working against the prince. Or that there was another dark wizard on your trail."

He looked highly uncomfortable at the idea, and for the first time since almost accidentally beating him to death Dylan seemed to sympathize.

"We don't know that for sure," he said quietly, "but we've faced a series of circumstances along the journey that have led us to believe there's a darker power at play. Working against us."

"Avalanches," Tanya volunteered.

"Rock slides," Cassiel added.

"The shape-shifter's cooking..."

The five of them turned to look at Rose, and she quickly dropped her head.

"The *point* is, Alwyn's been searching for him," Katerina steered the conversation back on track. "And I think Dylan's right. We should check in and see what he's found."

"The river's been following along at the base of these hills," Dylan explained, gazing out over the horizon. "We should be able to find a quiet spot to—"

"I don't like this idea."

Again, five pairs of eyes turned accusingly. This time they were locked on Aidan. The vampire flushed—as much as a vampire can flush—but held his ground. "It was one thing when we were rounding up rebels, but now you're dealing with sorcery." He eyed the stone warily. "And a contact on the inside you neglected to mention to Petra." There was a moment of hesitation before he shook his head. "As her proxy, I can't support this."

For a moment, all was silent. Then Dylan stepped forward with a broad smile.

"Of course, you can't," he replied in a surprisingly sympathetic tone. "If I was in your position, I wouldn't either." In a move that astonished them all he draped an arm over the vampire's shoulder as he began purposely leading him in the opposite direction. "And none of us is going to hold that against you. In fact, I admire you for standing your ground."

"What is this?" Aidan asked stiffly, running his tongue reflexively over his teeth.

"You are well within your rights to disagree, and you have my word that I'll support you when we get back to Pora." Dylan clapped him once on the shoulder, gesturing to the path back down the hill. "In the meantime, give Petra our best—"

The vampire suddenly dug in his heels, and even though Dylan was leading him swiftly in the opposite direction the two of them came to an abrupt stop. In a fluid gesture he slipped from beneath the ranger's arm, a caustic smile playing about his lips. "Oh, I see. You think I'm leaving, is that it?" His head tilted to the side, eyes dancing with dry amusement. "One disagreement and I head back to the camp? Leave you all on your own?"

Dylan sighed, not even bothering to deny it. "Well, you can't blame a guy for trying."

The vampire's smile sharpened as he turned around and headed back up the path. "Let's see if I can."

BY THE TIME THE GANG hiked to the bottom of the hills, the sun was beginning to dip lower in the sky. The river moved at a swift pace but scattered all along the pebbled banks were a hundred little inlets where Katerina could easily drop the stone. They wandered along a bit further, trying to find the perfect spot, before Dylan abruptly set down his satchel.

"Here's good." His eyes flickered over the thick reeds that sheltered their position before tossing Katerina the stone. "Remember, keep it quick. No need to be specific about our plans. Ask him about his. Where we right about there being another wizard? Was he able to track him down?"

No need to be specific about our plans? Katerina's lips curved up and she shot him a sarcastic smile. He may have used Aidan's mistrust of all things magic against him, but Dylan felt the same way. He was just as uncomfortable with the idea of dabbling in sorcery. Just as uneasy with placing his trust in a wizard as the vampire. *And to think, they could have used that to bond.*

"I'll do my best," she teased, sinking to her knees on the bank of the river.

The stone felt cool and heavy in her hand, and all at once a surge of excitement swept through her at the prospect of seeing Alwyn. She had so many things to ask him, so many things she'd discovered since their last talk. Did he know about her mother's power? Had he suspected that Katerina might have it as well? Perhaps most importantly...

...could she ask those things in front of all these people?

"Keep it simple and quick," Dylan reminded her quietly, his bright eyes roving reflexively around the open terrain. "This place is still a little too exposed for my taste."

The princess nodded and held the stone high above the water, her every thought centered on the wizard's winkled face. Knowing their luck, she would catch him in the middle of dinner. Or even worse, in some kind of council meeting. *That* might take some explaining.

Alwyn.

She said the name in her mind, her fingers curling around the stone. It dropped freely from her hand and fell into the gentle water, vanishing with hardly a splash. There was a moment of silence as each of the five friends leaned over the bank. Staring down into the quiet water. Waiting.

Then all hell broke loose.

"RUN!"

It was impossible to say who shouted first. One second, the world was blanketed in peaceful silence. The next, the entire thing had exploded in a wall of sound.

"Kat—RUN!"

The princess lifted her head in horror just as the first of the royal infantrymen burst through the trees. There were too many to count. They were yelling too loudly for her to think. Her eyes shot back to the water, and for a split second she thought she glimpsed Alwyn's face. Then a pair of strong hands grabbed her by the shoulders and she was hauled to her feet.

"Dylan!" she screamed, trying to make out his face in the blur of arrows, swords, and blood that followed. The edge of a blade whipped past her face, and she staggered back. "DYLAN!"

They were wildly outnumbered. That much was easy to see. Everywhere Katerina looked more and more soldiers were pouring down to the riverside, closing in around the circle of friends.

Metal was flashing, people were shouting, heavy curses flew. An earsplitting growl rumbled through the earth as a jet-black wolf dove into the fray. Within seconds, she was joined by another. This one was chocolate brown with a familiar pair of sky-blue eyes.

"Katerina, get down!"

The princess ducked just as a double-headed ax spiraled towards her, slicing through the air where her neck had been just seconds before. She looked up in time to see Cassiel racing towards her, a silver knife flashing in each hand, but he was quickly blocked by no fewer than seven men.

Get up! Don't just freeze! You've got training, too! Get up and fight!

With a sudden cry the princess pushed to her feet, snatching a blade from a fallen soldier and smashing it with all her might against the nearest guard. It hit him square in the back but bounced off his impenetrable armor. Not enough to hurt him. But it *was* enough to get his attention. A second later, he broke away from Cassiel and rounded on her.

The first strike she managed to dodge. The second hit her right in the face. A pool of blood burst in her mouth and she stumbled backwards, blinking away stars.

What am I doing? They're too experienced. I don't know what I'm doing.

Two weeks of lessons didn't account for the four years of hardcore training required to get into the royal reserve. The princess might have grasped the basics but she was far outmatched, and the next blow was sure to finish her off. She had only one hope to save her. And just like her newly-discovered shifter blood, it was tentative at best.

Your magic. Use your fire.

Katerina lifted her hands. She searched desperately for that upwelling of emotion that had summoned the flames last time. That out-of-body focus that had allowed her to tap into the latent power. But the magic eluded her. All she felt was fear.

When the soldier lunged again, she tripped back with a scream. He raised his sword, but before it could come down a silver arrow lodged in the base of his throat.

She looked up in shock to see Tanya standing on a bluff about twenty yards away. A shining bow raised in her slender hands. Firing out arrows with such speed and accuracy, they were nothing more than a blur. She saw the princess watching her, however, and had time to mouth a single word.

RUN!

Then she was overtaken by soldiers once more.

Katerina tried one more time with the fire. Tried to see past the waves of disorientation and terror and focus her thoughts, but it was no use. In the sea of death and bloodshed around her, she was as helpless as a child. A far cry from the dragon she'd been before.

She turned on her heel. Tried to find an opening in the soldiers to escape. But before she could take a step, something heavy crashed into her back. She fell to the ground, landing hard upon her palms as a pair of razor-sharp teeth sank into her sleeve. A wave of terror rushed over her but before she could pull in the breath to scream, a chocolate-colored wolf leapt right in front of her.

A soldier who'd been rushing towards her fell to the ground, his throat ripped to pieces before he had time to reach for his knife. Two more soon followed before the wolf slowly turned back around, shreds of bloody clothing dripping from his teeth.

The mayhem around them seemed to suspend as he and the princess locked eyes. Then he leapt forward and grabbed her by the sleeve once more, pulling her desperately towards the trees.

"Okay," she gasped, yanking herself free as her legs stumbled after him, "I'm going." Then a wave of icy terror froze in her veins and she blurted, "Come with me!"

There was no way he would survive if he went back. There was no way any of them could survive. Already, the peaceful riverbank was stained with a thick layer of blood. Swirls of crimson clouded the water, drifting slowly with the current. And while Cassiel was still standing, she could no longer see Rose. Tanya was gone as well, although Katerina couldn't see a body. She could only hope that the girl had shifted into someone else and was fighting them from their own side.

"Please," she whispered, grabbing hold of his thick fur. "Don't go. If you go, you might not come back. I might never see you again—"

Even as she said the words, a flash of metal whipped through the air and the giant wolf let out a tortured cry. Katerina gasped in horror, only to find an arrow wedged into the muscle beneath his shoulder. Something far different than the sleek silver arrows Tanya had been using. Something blunt and bronze. He turned his head with a wolfish glare as the archer reloaded his bow. He probably would have fired off the shot, too, if Cassiel hadn't suddenly impaled him from behind.

"Really?" the fae shouted, fending off five soldiers at once. "We're in the middle of a battle and you sneak away to make out with your girlfriend? You could at least shift back first..."

At his words, Katerina snapped out of her trance. Acknowledging the selfish undercurrents beneath her request. Knowing full well that he could never abandon the rest of them.

And I don't want him to. I just don't want him to die.

With a parting glance to the princess, Dylan took a step towards the fae. But the second he put weight on it, his leg buckled beneath him. He turned his head to bite out the arrow himself but was unable to reach it.

Pale as a ghost, Katerina stepped forward herself. "Here, I've got it."

With trembling fingers, she grabbed the arrow by the bloodied feathers and pulled with all her might. There was a rush of blood, but the thing barely budged an inch. She'd been wrong. It hadn't lodged in the muscle, it had embedded deep in the bone. Too far down for her to retrieve it.

"I'm sorry!" she cried, trying again and again. Torrents of blood spilled over her hands, but still the thing refused to come loose. "I'm so sorry! I'm trying, it's just—"

"Let me."

Katerina and Dylan looked up at the same time as a tall man swept towards them. His pale face stained red from the battle. His clothes ripped and torn. His razor-sharp fangs sinking into his lower lip. With a stab of guilt, the princess realized there was one person she'd forgotten to look for.

Aidan.

He took one look at the arrow, then sank to his knees by Dylan's side. If he was at all afraid of the giant teeth hovering just inches away from his neck, he didn't let on. Instead, he gripped the bloody projectile and braced his other hand against the wolf's shoulder.

"Hold still," he commanded.

One mighty pull and the arrow came loose. It dropped onto the ground between them as the vampire pushed swiftly to his feet. He didn't breathe like the rest of them, there were no panting breaths to cue them in, but it didn't take much to see he was tired. There was a distinct tenderness to the way he was holding one side of his body, and his fingers trembled as they raked back his hair.

"Are you okay?" he asked tersely, eyeing the wolf. "Can you walk?"

Dylan tested his leg gingerly then nodded, looking as close to embarrassed as was possible in his canine form. Aidan nodded stiffly and started heading back down the mountain. But before he could go more than a few steps, Dylan lunged forward and caught him by the sleeve.

"Dylan, what are you doing?" Katerina shrieked. Aidan looked down in astonishment, his eyes zeroing in on the wolf's lethal teeth. For a second it looked like he was going to forget himself completely and the two were going to fight it out right there, but then the wolf released him and stared intently into his eyes.

It was one of the strangest things the princess had ever seen. Amidst the flurry of the battle, the two were standing perfectly still. Locked in silent communication. Each dripping blood.

For a second, nothing happened. Then Dylan tilted his head towards Katerina and turned back to the vampire with a low whine. Aidan looked absolutely stunned. Twice he followed the gesture before, at last, he seemed to understand.

His back straightened, his jaw clenched, and he gave the wolf a stiff nod. A second later he was flying away into the woods, the princess gripped safely in his arms.

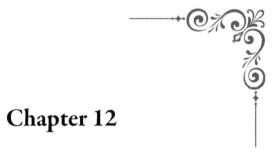

Chapter 12

Katerina didn't know how long she and the vampire ran through the woods. She stopped keeping track of time. The sun was setting when they left, and by the time they finally stopped it had sunk behind the thick canopy of trees, leaving the air chilled and wanting in its wake.

Gentle hands lowered her to the ground. Gentle fingers lifted her chin. Her eyes blinked open, and she found herself staring into a beautiful face. Pale as the stars and creased with concern.

"Are you all right?" he asked softly.

There was a brief pause. A moment where they simply stared. Then, in a move that would have been comical were it not for the horrors of the day, the princess sneezed a mouthful of blood.

...right into the vampire's face.

It was impossible to say who looked more surprised. For a second, they simply froze. Then Katerina clapped a hand over her mouth in horror, and Aidan looked down with the hint of a smile. He reached up to touch his cheeks, the tips of his fingers stained with blood.

"...bless you."

Then Katerina blacked out.

WHEN SHE AWOKE, SOMETIME later, it was clear that she'd been out for a while. The lighter swirls of navy in the sky had given way to an inky black. The moon had risen directly above them, and there was a small imprint in the ground where she'd been lying amongst the leaves.

Her eyes opened just a sliver, peering out from beneath her lashes, and she saw Aidan sitting by her side. His back was to her as he gazed out over the moonlit vista, but she could still see the wistful expression in his eyes. The soft nostalgia that swept over him as the wind blew back his hair.

The next instant, his shoulders tensed. He glanced behind him, meeting the princess' stolen gaze. She blushed but he offered a gentle smile, turning around to face her.

"I'm glad you're awake." His voice took on an almost musical cadence, lilting soothingly amongst the trees. "There's a good chance your friends would have killed me otherwise."

If they were even alive... Katerina's eyes flashed automatically back towards the river valley, but she banished the thought from her mind. They were alive. She knew it. They simply had to be.

"How did you do that?" she asked, changing the subject. A look of confusion flitted across his face, and she gestured out to the vista. "How did you know I was awake? You weren't looking."

"I heard your heart." He stuck his hands deep in his pockets, as if this was the most reasonable thing in the world. "They speed up when people wake."

The princess could think of nothing to say to this. In the end, she merely nodded and wrapped her cloak tighter around her as the two of them stared into the night.

Aidan had stopped on a little bluff overlooking the hills and valley below. They were still safe within the tree line, but at such a vantage point that they could see anyone approaching before that person could see them. It was a good spot. Dylan would have approved.

Katerina's heart clenched just thinking his name, and Aidan glanced over sharply. Maybe he could hear that, too.

"They're going to be all right, you know."

She glanced up in surprise to see him thoughtfully staring back. There was no hint of a lie on his face. He wasn't saying it just to make her feel better. There was just a calm reassurance.

"You don't know that."

She was surprised by how weak her own voice sounded, then wasn't surprised at the same time. Of course, it was. If there was one thing the day had taught her it was that she was undeniably, unforgivably, weak.

"No... but I'm as certain as I can be." His lips twitched up in a wry smile. "I happen to be something of an expert on death."

The princess failed to see the humor. He bowed his head with a sigh.

"But seriously, Katerina. I've been around a long time, and I can say without a hint of pride that your friends are some of the best fighters I've ever seen. Yes, they were outnumbered. But those kinds of odds either overwhelm you in the beginning, or they don't. All four of them made it through the initial attack. I'd be willing to bet they made it to the end as well."

In spite of her best efforts, the princess began to hope. It was impossible not to. There was something irresistibly convincing about his words. Something that made it impossible to doubt.

"At any rate, I can't imagine that Dylan will leave you alone with me too long." The vampire wrapped his arms around his knees and gazed back over the vista. "On the off-chance that I forget my manners entirely and turn you into some royal lollipop."

Katerina snorted in laughter, then glanced over at him with a grin. There was too much truth in the words to be entirely funny, but it was funny nonetheless.

"Is he your boyfriend?"

The word caught her off-guard. She'd used it several times herself, but only within the safe confines of her own mind. To hear someone else say it, casually as could be, was shocking.

"Yeah," she answered quietly, cheeks warming with a blush, "I guess he is."

Aidan studied her for a moment, then returned to the horizon with a little smile. "That makes sense. He's unbearably overprotective. And until today, I'd never received a wolfish SOS."

Again, Katerina couldn't help but grin. *Wolfish SOS?* It sounded like something Tanya would say. How could the others not see it? He was so much like them.

"I'm sorry about my friends..." she ventured tentatively, stealing another glance out of the corner of their eye. "I don't have much experience with vampires myself, but they all seem to have these preconceived notions—"

"Don't apologize," he said shortly. "I'm used to it."

It fell quiet between them once more as the subject was dropped. He was perfectly prepared to keep it that way. She was not.

"You saved my life," she ventured again, a little firmer this time. "You risked everything you had to help me, and then were almost beaten to death for your troubles."

The words washed over him without effect. It wasn't until she reached out suddenly and lay her hand upon his that he showed a spark of life.

"Aidan... *thank you.*"

His eyes widened almost imperceptibly as he glanced down at their hands in surprise. At first, he tensed to pull away, but after a second he seemed rather pleased. The same way his lips had curved up the second she called him by his name. "You're welcome."

They sat for a moment in awkward silence, little smiles still playing about their lips before he straightened up swiftly, raking his hair back in that same self-conscious gesture Dylan did himself.

"So how is it you don't have experience with vampires?" he asked conversationally. "Surely the king kept one or two in the dungeon for you kids to tear apart."

Katerina's head snapped up, but she relaxed when she saw the mischief dancing in his eyes. "Very funny," she replied, although she stifled a secret shudder wondering if any part of that was true. "I just don't. Besides the ones back at Pora, you're the only vampire that I've ever met. And those others didn't seem to like me very much."

Aidan laughed softly, as if the entire thing was just a fading memory. "I think the problem was that they liked you a little too much, but I see your point. You must have a lot of questions, then," he continued suddenly. "Ones I bet you've been too nervous to ask."

Under any other circumstances, the observation would have made her blush. But for whatever reason Katerina felt herself scooting closer, thrilled that someone finally understood.

She might have come a long way in the last few months, but at heart she was still that over-curious little girl who'd grown up in the castle. Completely astonished that all those magical creatures she'd read about in her stories had suddenly come to life...

"Well, to start... I'm actually a little surprised you can be out in sunlight."

Aidan nodded sagely and leaned back on his arms, stretching out his long legs as the two of them settled into the tall grass. "Yeah, that one's pretty popular. I think it comes from the pale skin. Vampires are a little sensitive to light, blame it on the heightened senses, but that's the extent of it. I can walk in the sun just the same as you."

Katerina nodded eagerly, trying to prioritize the flood of questions that had clambered to the forefront of her brain. "What about a stake through the heart?"

He laughed softly, dark hair falling into his eyes. "I imagine if you stab anything hard enough in the heart, you'll probably kill it."

Good point.

"Garlic?"

He opened his mouth to reply, then hesitated with a thoughtful pause. "You mean, do I not like garlic? Or do I not like it when the person I'm feeding on has eaten it recently?"

To him, it was a reasonable question. To her, it was a chilling reminder.

"Because I've got nothing against garlic by itself," he continued casually. "But, no, I'm not a big fan of it in my food."

His food. He means people. Ordinary, everyday people. People just like me.

They lapsed into silence again, the cheerful back-and-forth vanishing as they gazed out over the shadowy hills. It was several minutes before Katerina dared to speak once more.

"Is it hard for you?" she asked quietly, resisting the urge to pull her thick cloak higher up around her chin. "To control yourself, I mean. Being around so many people?"

For a second, Aidan looked incredibly sad. He glanced down at the bluish veins spidering her wrist, took a deep breath, and then raised his eyes. As calm as could be. "Yes."

It was a strange moment. One the princess would remember for as long as she lived. Perhaps the strangest thing about it was that, despite him confessing to a deeply ingrained desire to kill her whist the two were alone in the woods, Katerina felt not a hint of fear. Instead, she felt a strange kind of comradery. A kinship to him she couldn't explain.

Maybe it was the fact that they were both outsiders. Maybe it was the fact that they'd both been cursed with the legacy of their blood. Maybe it was just that he was so depressingly honest.

"So, I have a question for *you*." He leaned forward suddenly, his eyes glittering like black gemstones under the light of the stars. "You're rounding up all the rebels, right? Going from camp and camp?" Katerina nodded and he continued cautiously. "You never thought to round up the other people as well?"

"The other people?" she echoed curiously.

For the first time since they'd met, his face darkened with a hint of derision. "Maybe because you don't think of them as people."

Whoa, there—hold up!

"No, I'm sure I do," Katerina cut him off quickly. "I just don't know who—"

"How do you intend to rule the supernatural community," he interrupted quietly, "if you refuse to give them the option to fight for you?"

The princess stared at him in shock. She didn't think anyone had ever asked her that kind of question before. And, as it stood, she hadn't the faintest clue as to the answer.

"I'm giving people the option to fight," she answered hesitantly. "You saw the people in that camp, it's all different sorts—"

"No, it's a select few." He shook his head with a quiet sigh. "And that, my dear, is the heart of your problem. You don't know the answer to the question."

There was something infuriating about him, yet Katerina found it was impossible to be infuriated at the same time. Most likely because she had a sneaking suspicion that, whatever he was talking about, he was probably right.

"And what is the question?" she asked tersely. "Keep in mind, if you try to give me some riddle I'm going to try out that stake thing myself."

A faint smile flitted across his face before he leaned forward on his knees, staring intently into her eyes. "The question is... what do you have that can defeat your brother?"

Ironically enough, Katerina's first thought was her friends. Even though there were only five of them. Even though she didn't know if they were currently alive. Her next thought was her magic.

I can turn into a dragon. Rain down fire. Level the playing field with a single breath.

But just as quickly as she'd thought the words, her shoulders slumped with a miserable sigh.

"Nothing." Her gaze dropped to her lap as scenes from the battle flashed back in front of her eyes. "There's nothing I have that can defeat him."

The shock of the realization stopped her cold, and it was all she could do to keep from crying. What good was Alwyn, when he was so far away? What good were her friends, when there were only five of them against an entire kingdom? And what use were her ridiculous powers, when she couldn't even summon them at her time of need?

She half-expected Aidan to agree with her. At the very least, she expected him to be gracious enough to keep quiet. But he let her stew only a moment before rolling his eyes and asking again.

"Stop feeling sorry for yourself and answer the question."

She looked up in shock: half at the demand, half at his tone. "What are you talking about?" she replied, her voice rising in distress. "There's nothing I can do. You saw me today in the battle. I can't take care of myself, let alone anyone else."

Aidan's eyes twinkled as he leaned back with a little smile. "Just what you want to hear from your future queen."

"I'm *serious*, Aidan," she insisted. "You think I'm proud of it? I just spent the better part of a month getting my ass kicked trying to learn how to defend myself. It wasn't nearly enough. And the second I discovered these stupid powers, we had to leave—"

"Enough." He held up a hand to silence her. "I'm not talking about magic, or dragons, or spells, or how well you can level a broad sword. I'm talking about *you*." His eyes burned into her own, making it impossible to look away. "What do *you* have that your brother doesn't?"

There was a quiet pause. Then the answer slowly dawned on her.

"I have the will of the people."

He leaned back, looking satisfied, his eyes resting upon her with a hint of pride. "Yes, you do."

A sudden sense of calm swept over Katerina as she realized the quiet wisdom in his words, but there was something hidden beneath them as well. Something just as important.

Him. He's talking about himself, too.

It was suddenly clear to her. As clear as the reason Petra had sent him along.

There's a reason he saved me from the vampires. There's a reason he didn't fight back when the others dragged him into the woods. He's been trying to tell us something. He'd been fighting for his own race.

We've just been too prejudiced to listen.

"I don't think Dylan, or... I've never met a vampire like you," she said slowly, weighing each word as she stared at him intently. "Are there others?"

Aidan nodded slowly, meeting her searching eyes. "More than you'd think," he answered automatically. Then he amended with a quiet sigh. "I mean... there are others willing to try."

The princess nodded, silently absorbing this as the two leaned away from each other and turned back to the moonlit view. Her mind was churning and his face was impossible to read, but for the first time in what seemed like ages she felt as though she had somewhere to start.

Maybe they were going about this the wrong way. Maybe what they needed was a single unifying sign—not a series of smaller alliances. And maybe, by the time it was all done, the vampires would have earned themselves a seat at the table.

Only time would tell. But, if today was any indication, time was no longer on their side.

"Oh, and Aidan?" she added suddenly. "You asked what I had that could defeat my brother? Well, I don't know what Petra told you, but I can turn into a dragon."

The vampire turned towards her for a moment, staring in disbelief, then his charming face softened with a burst of laughter that echoed off the trees. "Sure, you can, princess. So can I."

THE TWO DIDN'T SPEAK anymore for the next few hours. Katerina dozed fitfully at the base of a cedar while Aidan kept steady watch, appearing to require very little sleep himself. It wasn't until the sky lightened with the faintest hints of dawn that there was a sudden rustling in the trees.

It woke her out of a light sleep, stealing her breath and stopping her heart all in the same moment. Her eyes had just snapped open, when a hand clamped over her mouth, dragging her out of sight as easily as if she were a doll. A second later, she was stashed deep in the leaves.

"Who's there?" Aidan called cautiously, his sharp eyes scanning the forest. When no one replied he called again, a little louder. "Show yourself!"

"Would you look at that," a familiar voice called back. "Seems our pet vampire has got himself a little spooked. Jumping at shadows and whatnot."

Dylan.

Katerina's heart lifted in her chest as she leapt to her feet.

"It seems a bit counterintuitive," Tanya answered, "for a vampire to be afraid of the dark." Her face tightened with a little frown. "Maybe we should ask for our money back."

"No," Cassiel replied patiently, "that's why you *train* them. Vampires are an investment. You can't expect perfection the first time around."

Aidan rolled his eyes and relaxed his position with a sullen glare, while Katerina went running forward. She didn't slow her pace until she had leapt into Dylan's arms.

"Hey, you." He caught her with a wide grin, checking her discreetly for damages and far more pleased than he was letting on. "Miss me?"

Both he and Rose were ironically dressed in the colors of the royal infantry. Apparently, they hadn't been able to salvage any of their own clothes in their hurry to shift. The others still looked exactly as they had that morning, despite being doused in a few dozen gallons of blood.

"No time to miss you.; I happened to have some *great company*," she replied, giving him a punishing swat to the chest. He took the hint immediately and lowered her gently to the ground, crossing the space between himself and the vampire in just three long strides.

"Thank you," he said without preamble. He might not have extended his hand, but sincere gratitude was ringing in every word. "I owe you a great deal, Aidan. I won't forget it."

It was the first time he'd said the vampire's name, and this alone produced a great effect.

Aidan's eyes lightened with surprise and his face softened with the hint of a smile before he lifted a shoulder in a casual shrug. "It was no problem."

Katerina rolled her eyes then leapt onto Tanya and Cassiel, engulfing each one of them in a giant, unsolicited hug. They were battered and bloody but beaming nonetheless. Just a step behind them, Rose couldn't stop bouncing up and down—oblivious to the sea of twigs caught in her hair.

"Okay, so what's next?" she asked, equally unaware that every time she opened her mouth one of her lips split back open and started bleeding. "Shall we track down more of them? Slaughter another company or two? I, for one, was just getting warmed up—"

"*Now* we sleep," Dylan interrupted, though he gave her an indulgent smile. His arm was still fastened safely around Katerina's waist, and there was little chance of it leaving any time soon. "But if you still feel that way in the morning, I promise I'll let you lead the way."

An empty promise. Katerina knew they were going to feel a lot like death in the morning.

The others chuckled and stared around the little campsite, slowly taking off their weathered gear as they prepared to settle in for the night.

Only Rose remained where she was standing, revved high on adrenaline, and completely unable to come down. "Sleep," she scoffed. "How could you even think of sleep at a time like this?"

TEN MINUTES LATER, the entire camp was passed out cold. They had been too tired to even select a lookout. Too worn out by the events of the day to do anything more but close their eyes.

However, as it turned out, *sleep* was not meant to be...

Chapter 13

Katerina heard it before she saw it. Drifting down through the campsite on the wings of a dream. A sound so painfully sweet and beautiful it brought the sting of tears to her eyes. A sound so tangible and real it was almost as if she could reach out and touch it—snatch the lilting melody right off the gentle breeze.

Around her, the others were waking. Not all of them, but some.

Rose was lost in a slumbering coma, twitching every now and then the way shifters were prone to do in their sleep. Tanya was lying right beside her, out like a light. Aidan was stirring but didn't wake. His forehead was creased with tension, as if he was having a bad dream.

But as Katerina lay there in stunned silence, she watched the power of the music take effect.

Dylan and Cassiel opened their eyes at the same time, blinking sleepily as if they were lost in a daze. They took no notice of each other but lifted their heads to peer in wonder at the night sky, the dazzling starlight reflecting like a mirror in their bright eyes. For a moment they simply lay there, seemingly overwhelmed. Then, at the same time, they pushed gracefully to their feet.

"You guys," Katerina whispered, scrambling up as well. She didn't know why exactly she was lowering her voice, but something about the music seemed to demand it. Seemed to require a reverential respect. "What's going on? What is that sound?"

It was like they couldn't even hear her. Cassiel bypassed her completely, turning his head to gaze down in the direction of the river. Dy-

Ian offered her a blank smile before doing the same. The music picked up speed the second they did. Less of a lullaby, and more of a call. The high, plaintive notes beseeching them to come closer. For them to find the voice behind the song.

The men were more than happy to oblige.

Without a moment's pause they headed straight out of the campsite, leaving the others lying on the ground behind them. Cassiel actually walked on Tanya's outstretched hand, but he didn't seem to notice any more than Dylan noticed he was heading out into the cold without a shirt.

"Guys?" Katerina called again, her voice rising in alarm. The music changed itself to counter her noise, rising and falling like the waves of a tide. Pulling them ever closer.

It wasn't until they disappeared into the shadows that her feet unfroze from the ground and she had the sense to move. Snatching up a dagger from Dylan's discarded belt she took off after them, tearing through the underbrush with a lot less grace and a lot more noise.

Both the ranger and fae were accustomed to the forest, moving swiftly through the trees. But, although Katerina had a hard time following them, it was easy to guess exactly where they were going. She'd guessed it the very first moment those sweet notes dripped down through the trees.

They were going to the river.

The world itself was in transition. Caught between the departing glow of moonlight and the rising promise of a new dawn. Katerina scurried down the forest path as quickly as she could, illuminated occasionally by the fading light of stars. Twice, the long skirt of her dress got caught in the underbrush and slowed her down. Twice, she went sprawling onto the forest floor.

Perhaps, if that hadn't happened, she would have gotten there in time. Perhaps, if that hadn't happened, things might have been different. As it stood the princess burst out of the trees and onto the shoreline, only to stumble upon a truly unforgettable scene.

Dylan Aires... kissing a beautiful woman in the moonlight.

Katerina stopped dead in her tracks, as if the strings that connected her arms and legs had been cut straight through. She blinked twice. Tried to reconcile it. Tried to make it make sense. But, when she opened her eyes a moment later, it was still happening.

The love of her life had his arms wrapped around another woman, his sky-blue eyes closed in a deep and leisurely kiss.

"Dylan?"

She could barely force the word out. Barely make her voice louder than a whisper. Not that it mattered. It was if he was someplace he couldn't hear her, caught in the inescapable embrace of that haunting song. The woman looked up, though. Her eyes danced with a wicked smile.

Cassiel was standing just a few feet away. His arms wrapped around not one woman, but two. The first reached up and unwound the leather band in his hair, spilling it long and silver down his shoulders. He made a compulsive movement, as if to pull away, but she wound a hand around the back of his neck with a seductive smile. The song got louder. He didn't even seem to notice when yet a third woman came up behind him and started taking off his coat.

"Guys... snap out of it." Katerina's voice was shaking. Every part of her was shaking. But she couldn't, for the life of her, seem to move. It was as if whatever force had called them down to the river had a hold on her, too. Only, it wasn't seducing her. It was making her watch. *"Please."*

The 'please' broke through to Dylan.

His eyes fluttered open, and for a second it looked like he was coming up for air. A little shiver swept over his body as his blue eyes flickered to Katerina's stricken face, but before he could open his mouth to speak a pair of soft red lips started whispering in his ear.

A visible wave of relaxation took hold, and Katerina watched with wide eyes as he forgot about her entirely and took a step into the river. Then another. Then another after that.

Seven hells... An icy chill took hold of the princess, settling in painful little shards deep in her stomach. *She's going to drown him...*

"Dylan!" she screamed aloud, her voice echoing over the stillness of the water.

Cassiel continued his walk into the river, a dreamlike enchantress gripping lightly onto each wrist, but for the second time Dylan seemed to falter.

Streaks of moonlight and shadows fell across his bare chest as he detached himself from the woman and turned his face back to shore. His eyes swept over Katerina, and for a moment it was almost like he could see her. For a moment, it was like the curtain between them fell away.

"Dylan, get away from her! It's a trap!"

A faint shadow flickered across his face, clouding the edges of that dazed serenity. A cognitive dissonance so great it almost looked as though he was in pain. But the woman had reached her limit with Katerina's meddling. And she was not about to lose her prize.

"Dylan," she repeated, saying his name for the first time. A glassy sheen fell over his bright eyes as he turned back to her. "What a lovely name..."

That eerie melody danced around them, hanging heavy in the air.

He held perfectly still as the woman stretched up on her toes and kissed his lips. Her fingers trailed down his bare chest. Her hair wrapped around him in little tendrils, holding his arms. For a moment, it was as if he was a statue. Then, all at once, a part of him came to life. His hands tangled in her wild hair, tilting her face up to his. Then just kissing wasn't enough and those hands drifted lower, playing with the edge of her dress. A secret smile of satisfaction danced across her face as she backed a step away, into deeper water. He hesitated a moment, then followed.

"DYLAN!"

Just a few yards away, Cassiel was already up to his chest. A layer of tension had settled in his shoulders, and although he continued kissing the woman he seemed to be under duress. The other two circled around him, like birds orbiting their prey. Every now and then, one would reach up and twirl a lock of his hair. Lick the side of his face. Whisper deadly nothings in his ear.

"Dylan! Cass is in trouble!" Katerina shrieked. Maybe, if his love for her couldn't snap him out of it, his fear for his friend would. "They're pulling him under! He's going to drown!"

Dylan turned his head in the fae's direction but the woman grabbed his face with deceptive strength, forcing him to look at her instead. A shudder ran through his body, but he held her gaze.

"Come with me," she whispered in his ear, the tip of her tongue grazing his skin. "You know that you want to..."

Cassiel was up to his shoulders. His pale hair trailing out in the water. The woman who'd ensnared him still glued to his mouth, her legs circling his waist. Katerina screamed again and threw her body towards the water, but her feet were glued to the spot.

"Come with me."

The words whispered in the air, tickling the princess' ears and seeping deep into her subconscious. Dylan pulled in a shaking breath, swaying slightly on his feet.

"...no," he answered quietly, but he took a step with her into the water. "I don't—"

"Yes, you do," she soothed, running her fingers through his hair. His neck turned to follow every gesture—a man trapped in a dream. "Everyone does. Eventually." She leaned back suddenly and looked him over with a speculative smile. "Even men who are already in love."

Katerina threw herself forward once more and fell to her knees. She felt as though her heart was breaking. She didn't have the strength to scream. She didn't have the strength to cry. She simply watched as the man she'd fallen in love with walked forward to die.

Cassiel was up to his neck. His body was shaking, but he'd fallen into that same dreamlike trance. He was so far gone he didn't even notice it was getting hard to breathe.

"In love..." Dylan echoed in a daze. The woman bit his lower lip with an evil grin. "I can't do this... I can't—"

"Yes, you can," she said a bit more firmly. The music swelled around them as if to drive the point home. "You can, and you will. You want to." She stroked a finger along the edge of his cheek, lips curving up in a disturbingly affectionate smile. "And I do, too. That's rare."

Both hands slipped down to his, pulling him deeper into the water.

"I think I'll have a little fun with you first..."

A broken sob welled up in Katerina's chest, choking her as she cringed against the wet bank of the shore. The world around her was flickering on and off. It was like, the closer Dylan got to death, she got one step closer, too. Like she could feel that icy water on her own skin, snaking its way up to her throat—

A sudden scream echoed through the air. Followed by another, more wretched than the first.

The princess lifted her head off the ground in time to see a silver blade whip past her. It flipped over twice before burying itself in the chest of one of the beautiful women still standing on the bank. Two more were already lying on the ground beside her. Staring up with lifeless eyes.

A flash of shadow followed the silver, and the next thing she knew Aidan was standing by her side. He took one look at the scene in front of him before his face darkened to something grim.

"Sirens."

He said the word as a curse, baring his fangs as a swarm of beautiful women streaked towards him. Their lips curling back in fearsome snarls. Their nails elongating into sharpened claws. The smooth curves of their once-beautiful faces growing so extreme and angular the bones themselves seemed to break through their skin.

Katerina screamed and cringed helplessly against her invisible ties as they fell around her like dominoes. Contorted and writhing. Lips curled back as they drew in a final, rattling breath.

The fight was quick but brutal. The women were as terrifying as they come, but they were no match for a vampire. Aidan made quick work of them. Using his hands instead of his fangs. His knife instead of his inborn strength. It wasn't until the very end, when the last of the women leapt upon his back, that he spun her around, parted his lips, and ripped out her throat with his teeth.

The song spluttered and died. Bringing an end to Katerina's paralysis with it.

"Dylan!" she shrieked, rushing forward into the water. It was littered with the bodies of dead sirens. Cold and frothing with blood. "Aidan, get Cass! He's already under!"

The fae's head had slipped beneath the crimson waves. There wasn't a sign of him or the three sirens that had taken him down. But Katerina couldn't think about that now. She couldn't be in two places at once—she'd have to relinquish that responsibility to Aidan.

In the meantime, she had her own man to save.

"Dylan!" She lunged forward in the water and grabbed hold of him, wrapping her shaking arms around his shoulders from behind. "There you are! I didn't—"

She froze, suddenly rigid. Realizing why he hadn't turned around. Understanding why his entire body had gone still as a statue. Seeing the serrated dagger pressed against his neck.

It seemed a few sirens had escaped Aidan's violent purge. The ones already in the water.

The woman hadn't fully transformed the same as her fallen sisters; there was still a look of wild beauty to her. But that beauty was overwhelmed with rage. A dark, frenzied sort of rage that sparked in her eyes as she turned her glare from Dylan to Katerina.

"If I'd known you were going to be this much trouble, I would have taken my time," she hissed. "Played with him a little. Made you both *feel* it."

A wave of nausea rocked through Katerina as she pictured the two of them kissing. Their lips passionately locked together. Her pointed nails winding through his hair...

"I'm surprised you actually have a weapon," Katerina said viciously, still holding tight to Dylan's shoulders. "Although, I can't imagine where you had to stash it in that dress."

"Oh, this?" The siren pressed in the point deeper, until it drew a trickle of blood. "I had all but forgotten. You see, I don't need a weapon to make your man fall in love with me."

There was a sarcastic pause.

"...you literally had to put him under a spell."

"Kat," Dylan interjected mildly, "let's not insult the nice woman until she's put *down* the knife she's holding to my neck."

"He wasn't easy, I'll give you that." The siren's eyes swept him up and down with a wistful sigh. "And I can understand the attraction. The two of you might have actually had the real thing."

Her eyes flashed a violent shade of crimson as her fingers tightened on the blade.

"But now we'll never know..."

It was in that moment that a few things happened at once.

Aidan pulled Cassiel out of the water, dragging him backwards as the fae fought for consciousness, giant scratches running along the length of his face. Dylan pulled in a quick breath, his piercing eyes freezing upon the blade. And Katerina remembered she had a blade of her own.

There was a flash of silver, followed by a cry of surprise.

The next second the siren was falling back into the murky water, the princess' knife wedged deeply in her chest.

"No," Katerina said quietly, staring down at her lifeless body. "I guess you won't."

The second the last siren fell, the chaos around them suddenly stilled. The birds stopped screaming. The wind quieted its gusts and gales. The river calmed and went peacefully on its way, slowly clearing the crimson waves back to a deeper shade of blue.

In a way, it was like the entire thing had never happened.

...except it most definitely had.

"Katerina!"

Dylan whirled around and grabbed her hands. Pale as a ghost. Wet and trembling. A streak of pink lipstick smeared across his face. For a split second it looked like he wanted to reach out and hold her, but an abstract fear held him back. Instead, he stared silently into her eyes. Too afraid to speak. Too uncertain to know what to say.

"Kat, I didn't..." He trailed off, blinking drops of water from his eyes. "I'm *so* sorry. You have to know that I would never—"

She silenced him with a kiss. A kiss that grew bolder and deeper as he slowly convinced himself she wasn't going to pull out the blade and use it on him next. When they finally stepped away from each other, he looked a little overwhelmed.

"I know," she said simply.

And that was that.

The fae was a slightly different story.

His siren experience had obviously progressed past the seduction stage and entered the phase where the beasts tried to drown him beneath the waves. No matter how long he lay upon the shore, he seemed unable to catch his breath. And, judging by the traumatized way his eyes kept flashing to the river, there was a chance his sex drive had been killed for good.

"Hey, buddy," Dylan said with a hint of amusement, making his way out of the water and onto the shore. "You okay?"

It certainly didn't look that way. His face was even paler than Dylan's, streaked every so often with bright- red gashes where the sirens had slashed at him with their nails. Strangely enough, Aidan bore a few of the same marks. Although his looked as though they'd been made with a set of much larger hands...

He saw them looking and rolled his eyes, wringing out his tunic into a puddle on the ground.

"Courtesy of your friend," he explained with a wry smile. "He thought I was trying to drown him." His hand drifted up to the marks with a wince. "The thought *did* cross my mind..."

The fae was too distraught to process much of anything going on around him, but Dylan stepped carefully forward, looking the vampire up and down with curious eyes.

"Why didn't it affect you—the siren's call?"

Aidan shot him a quick look before returning to his clothing. "Their call only works on the living. Vampires are technically dead."

They're not living creatures... don't even have a soul.

Dylan's words from before echoed accusingly between them, and Katerina shot him a superior smirk. He dropped his eyes quickly and hurried to attend to Cassiel.

"Well, isn't that convenient."

BY THE TIME THEY MADE it back to camp—Cassiel muttering something about 'sea witches' the entire time—the sun had just risen up above the trees. The others were stirring in their blankets but were none the wiser as Katerina and the men plopped down on the ground beside them.

According to Aidan, the call only worked upon women if they were currently preoccupied with the man it concerned. Given how often the ranger turned up in Katerina's dreams, she wasn't at all surprised that when the devils called for him she awoke as well.

The others had remained blissfully unaware.

"Well, good mooooorning." Tanya awoke with a lazy stretch, inadvertently flexing the fingers Cassiel had stomped on just an hour before. "I hope you guys slept better than I did. I had the world's officially worst dream."

"What was that, honey?" Cassiel sank down instantly beside her, wrapping an arm around her waist. The man wasn't exactly prone to pet names, but he'd been badly shaken and was desperate for her not to see. Not to mention, he was dealing with some pretty crippling guilt.

"It was about you, actually." She shot him an instant smile, resting her head automatically against his shoulder. "I dreamt you were cheating on me with some whore you met down by the river. The two of you were actually getting pretty intense by the time I woke up."

For a split second the entire camp went comically still. Then Cassiel pulled her gently into his lap, resting his cheek against her forehead as he stroked her waves of cinnamon hair. "Just a dream, babe." He shot the others a fierce look of warning that contrasted hilariously with the gentle tones of his voice. "Just a dream."

"Yeah."

She closed her eyes with a contented smile, and for a fleeting moment all was well.

"...why are you all wet?"

Chapter 14

The gang had no desire to stay in the river country once the story about the sirens got out. A rather predictable turn of events that took about fifteen minutes. Neither did they want to go back to the water and retrieve the stone—considering that most such magical devices were only good for one or two uses anyway. Dylan was all for hiking through the forest and taking the long way to get to Rorque, but Katerina had a different idea in mind. One that kept her thinking off by herself until the six of them finally stopped for lunch.

"When we get to Rorque, we have to remember to refill this little thing." Tanya squinted into the bottom of her trusty flask. "I'm down to my last drop."

"I'll remind you, sweetheart," Cassiel volunteered quickly.

"Don't talk to me."

Rose chuckled and settled herself down on the rocks, tilting back to expose her rather impressive breasts whilst soaking in every drop of sunlight. "This is why it's dangerous to form attachments to just one person," she said wisely, shooting Tanya a backwards glance. "You should do what I do—keep things fresh. Never stay too long with just one person."

The shape-shifter's eyes narrowed as she fixed her boyfriend with a shrewd stare. "I'm seriously considering it."

"Come on, Tan—it was a *spell*."

With that, the once-happy couple digressed into the day's ninth fight, and the others quickly made themselves scarce. Rose went off to get wood for the fire, Aidan slipped away to find himself a rabbit or some other unlucky prey, while Dylan and Katerina wandered quietly through the trees.

"Are you okay?" he finally asked, glancing down at her with concern. "You've barely said a word all day." Before she could answer he blurted, "You're not still angry about the siren thing, are you? Because if you are, I *completely* understand. But Cass is right. We were under a spell—"

"I'm not mad about the siren thing," Katerina assured him, quoting his words with a soft smile. "I'm just... wondering if we're on the right track here. If we came up with the right plan."

"What do you mean?" He pulled them both to a stop, staring at her with a frown. "Getting the camps on board is going to be critical if we want to have any shot—"

"No, I know that." Her crimson hair danced in the breeze as she gazed around the silent forest, wondering if what she was considering was even possible, wondering what the man in front of her was going to say. "Dylan, you trust me, don't you?"

"The five words every man fears..."

"I'm serious." She reached out and took his hand, squeezing gently. "You trust me?"

He was quiet for a moment, staring deep into her eyes, then he said without an ounce of hesitation, "I'd trust you with my life."

A surge of heat shot through her, radiating from the inside. Her skin flushed hot then cold, sending little shivers through her body as her face warmed with a radiant smile. "Good, because that's kind of what I'm asking..."

KATERINA'S GOAL WAS simple.

She didn't just want to get the rebels on board, those people who had already committed themselves to the cause. She wanted to extend the offer to the entire kingdom. To unite the entire supernatural community. Leaving no one left wanting. No one left out in the cold.

This meant a new idea. Coming at the same premise with a bit of a twist.

They didn't have time to go from camp to camp. The army was already everywhere, and there was no telling when her brother would decide to strike. The concept of going from camp to camp was also too small. If Katerina wanted to unite the entire countryside she'd need a gesture that was big enough for the task. One that would reach all the people, no matter what they were.

And she had just the gesture in mind...

"Are you sure you want to do this?" Cassiel asked for the tenth time, hovering nervously at the edge of the forest while Katerina bowed her head in silence, trying to concentrate. "I feel like we haven't exhausted all our options yet. There could be a dozen other ways to—"

"Shut up."

Dylan, Tanya, and Rose all said it at the same time, turning their backs on the fae as they focused on the princess instead. Only the vampire was hovering on the sidelines, just as confused as when they'd first started discussing things an hour before.

"I still wish someone would tell me what the heck is going on," he started.

"Quiet!" the others chorused back to him. "Leech," Rose added with a sneer.

Aidan rolled his eyes and fell silent, while Katerina stared down at the forest floor. She had been standing there for the last twenty minutes. Wrapped only in Dylan's travelling cloak. Preparing herself both mentally and physically for what was about to come.

Then the sun slipped beneath the trees. Her moment had arrived.

"All right everybody," she murmured, spreading her arms wide. "Stand back."

Please let this work. Please let this work.

The others backed automatically to the other side of the clearing, pulling the vampire with them by the back of the jacket. He protested and squirmed while Cassiel said a silent prayer.

"I don't get it," he snapped irritably. "What is this big gesture she's supposed to—"

There was a mighty roar then a dragon sprang up in their midst.

Tanya and Rose let out an automatic cheer. Dylan stared up at his girlfriend with a look of spellbound wonder in his eyes. Cassiel leaned hard against a tree, debating whether he was going to throw up. And Aidan jumped back like someone had sprayed him with holy water.

"WHAT THE BLOODY HECK IS THAT?!"

Katerina shrugged a scaly shoulder with a sharp-toothed grin.

I told you I could turn into a dragon.

As shocked as he was, the vampire seemed to read her exact thoughts.

"I thought it was a metaphor!" he shouted. "Something about a vulnerable young woman finding her inner strength—*seven hells*!" He sank down into a crouch. "That's a freakin' dragon."

"Finally." Cassiel forgot for a moment that he detested vampires and came to stand by Aidan's side. "Someone who agrees with me."

Katerina rolled her eyes and stomped her foot impatiently, inadvertently toppling a young cedar. The fae glanced between her and tree accusingly, while Dylan walked up to her with a smile.

"You ready for this?" He grabbed his fallen cloak off the ground, slipping it into the leather satchel hanging from his arm. "It's a big move. Can never be undone."

That's the idea.

Katerina nodded her head and sank down onto her knees, lowering a crimson wing onto the ground by his side. He stared at it for a moment before flashing her a sudden grin.

"You know I love this part, right?"

She rolled her eyes and nipped playfully at his heels as he leapt gracefully onto her back. The girls were soon to follow. In the end all that was left were Aidan and Cassiel, standing side by side.

"Wait a second..." The vampire stared with wide eyes, unable to look away. "We're supposed to get on that thing? Ride on her back? *Fly*?!"

"Not if the two of us stand our ground," Cassiel muttered under his breath.

"Are you coming, or what?" Tanya called tauntingly from her high perch. "You know, we're sweeping all of the five kingdoms tonight. You guys might have a hard time finding us by the time we decide to land."

One last look of indecision, then the vampire tentatively stepped forward. He eyed Katerina warily—probably uncomfortable with the idea of any creature with fangs bigger than his own—then offered up the world's most cautious smile.

"You remember that I saved your life, right? And your boyfriend's? Twice?"

She stared at him steadily, projecting as much reassurance as possible with her eyes. Whether or not it worked, she would never know. But a second later the vampire leapt on board with the others, leaving just one final person standing on the ground.

"Cass, get up here!"

The fae closed his eyes in a final grimace, then walked forward with a scowl. "Just knock me out. Wake me up when it's over."

KATERINA HADN'T KNOWN what she'd been expecting when she suggested the long flight. She hadn't known how to gauge a reaction, she hadn't even known if her own body would be up to the task. But soaring through the glorious twilight, stretching out her wings over the five kingdoms...

...she knew she'd made the right choice.

My kingdoms, she thought with a fiery smile, *my people*.

With a wild cry, she threw back her head and let loose a wave of liquid fire. A flaming arc so blinding and vibrant, it lit up the night as far as the eye could see. The sounds of distant screaming echoed from behind her—mostly coming from the vampire and the fae—and she surged forward with a smile. Doing it again, and again, and again.

Never had she felt so unrestrained. Never had she felt so truly alive. A surge of energy was coursing through her, sparking over her skin and setting her very blood on fire.

My kingdom. My people.

She couldn't stop saying it. Nor could she help the sudden feeling of pride as she soared over mountains and lakes, over villages and rivers, over the high frozen plains, and down into the heart of the woodland realm. Every city. Every kingdom. Every citizen staring up at her with wide, wondrous eyes. They were all hers.

Mine to protect. Mine to defend.

With a mighty roar, she let loose another wave of fire. This one was even brighter than the ones that had come before. It lit the sky from the east to the west. From the north to the south. From the rebel camps all the way to the edges of the royal territory, illuminating the lonely spire of a castle, resting on the very edge of the moonlit sky.

For a split second, she was tempted.

Why not just fly over there right now, perch on the roof of the eastern wing, and set fire to Kailas' bedroom? What was stopping her from doing that?

Her muscles coiled and the tips of her wings tilted slightly off course, steering them towards her childhood home, a low rumble of fire building in her chest.

Then she felt a gentle squeeze on the base of her neck and dropped her head with a sigh.

Why wasn't she doing those things? Because she wanted a monarchy, not a massacre. She wanted a castle, not a tomb. A kingdom, not a mass grave.

With a sudden twist of her wings they were heading north instead, towards the farthest reaches of the kingdom. A place she had never been. The plan was to seek shelter in an off-the-grid village, keep their ears low to the ground, and wait.

Wait to see what kind of reaction her midnight flight had on the people. Wait to see what groups were willing to rally to her side. Wait for Aidan's envoys to the vampires. Wait for Petra and the others to spread the word and swell the rebellion from the ground up.

Wait—that was the plan.

The plan, however, was soon to change...

WHERE DID KATERINA and her friends end up that night, but a tavern.

She sank onto the sticky booth with a welcome feeling of familiarity. She was starting to see why every friend she'd made in the supernatural world considered the local bar to be a second home. There was something comfortingly similar about each one. A place where they could immerse themselves in the company of people, but still be completely alone. A place where they could watch without being watched—to listen in secret, to drink and make plans.

And tonight certainly didn't disappoint.

"—saw it with my own eyes! A *dragon*—big as you could believe! Raining down fire and hell stone and all that!"

"They say it's the princess, the one who went missing. They say she's coming back to challenge her brother because she's the rightful heir to the throne."

"Well, she may be the rightful heir, but she's also a shifter. One of us."

"She's a *Damaris*, Randall."

"Yeah, but one of us! A *dragon*, no less! You ask me to choose between her and the prince... you can bet what my answer's going to be!"

Petra worked fast. So did her vast network of spies. In every tavern they'd stopped, in every random village, there was little talk of anything else.

"Well, I'd have to say our little flight was a great success." Tanya clinked her glass against the others', offering each a congratulatory smile. "To raising hell! May it always be on our terms."

"To raising hell."

They lifted their glasses, downing the shot of burning whiskey at the same time. The only one left out was the vampire sitting at the edge of the table, lost in thought.

"Sorry about that," Dylan apologized with a spiteful smirk. "You're so quiet, sometimes it's easy to forget about your specific dietary needs..."

Okay—that's it.

"You know what," Katerina snapped, "in the spirit of this supernatural unity we've been championing—how about you go and buy him a drink. All of you," she added with a fierce glare, cocking her head towards the bar. "He can tell you what he likes."

It might have had something to do with the fact that she was recently a dragon but the table emptied as quickly as a sieve, leaving only the princess and the shape-shifter left sitting.

"Sorry," Tanya apologized briskly when Katerina shot her a disbelieving glance. "I just assumed that didn't apply to me."

The princess rolled her eyes and leaned back in the booth, watching with a glare as Dylan awkwardly led the vampire to the bar, gesturing to the bottles with a rather sheepish expression.

"He knows that unprovoked hostility isn't the most attractive quality, right?"

Tanya followed her gaze, then set down her whiskey with a soft smile. "Kat, what's the one thing Dylan values above every other?"

The princess paused in surprise, then glanced at him again.

"My safety."

Tanya nodded slowly, an unexpectedly thoughtful look on her face.

"There isn't a person in this room who doesn't know at least five people who were killed by vampires. For walking down the street. For sitting too close to them at a bar." Their eyes drifted automatically towards Aidan, perched on a tavern stool. "It seems harsh and unprovoked? It's not. The first thing I learned out here on my own is to not take dumb risks. A vampire is just about the dumbest risk you can take."

Katerina listened with wide eyes, trying to reserve judgment, but finding herself oddly compelled at the same time. The girl saying the words was fearless, yet she was saying them. And in the few months since the princess had left the castle, she'd almost been killed by vampires twice.

"He seems nice enough," Tanya continued quietly. "He's sexy, too—but then, he would be. That's how they get you. They lure you in. Tell gentle lies. Make you feel safe. They stare at you with those dreamy eyes and then..."

She smacked her hand upon the table, soliciting a royal shriek.

"And then they suck the life out of you," she finished proudly. "It's just what vampires do."

Katerina flashed her a dirty look for the scare, but underneath it all she felt herself deeply troubled. She thought about how persuasive Aidan had been after the battle. The whole dragon flight was basically his idea. She thought about the way he'd seemed to look inside of her, see into the depths of her soul. How she'd scooted closer on the grass. Unable to stop. Unable to look away.

"Rose hasn't even flirted with him," Tanya concluded decisively, pouring herself another drink. "If you don't believe me, believe that. She's the world's best litmus test for crazy."

Bold words, coming from a girl who was using a goblin prison shank to hold up the curls of her hair, but Katerina decided to keep that opinion to herself. There was plenty else to think about.

Don't worry about Aidan. The guy saved your life. And Dylan's. And Cassiel's. And, yes, he might have been persuasive about the flight, but you agreed with it. Look around—it was clearly the right call.

Before she could clear her mind, the crowd parted and the rest of their party slid quickly back down onto the bench. Dylan and Cassiel were deliberately averting their eyes, Rose didn't look bothered by anything in particular, and Aidan was gripping a glass of blood, looking quite smug.

"So, Cass and I were talking," Tanya began with no preamble, "after I forgave him for being such a slut with the sirens. We decided that your midnight gesture isn't going to be enough."

Katerina looked up in surprise, while Dylan flashed the fae a questioning look.

"When the heck did you guys talk? I thought you were passed out for most the flight."

"I was," Cassiel admitted. "But when I came 'round, she got to me. And she's absolutely right." His dark eyes leveled on Katerina, holding her breathless with his steady gaze. "Yes, getting the people on your side is a good start, but it isn't going to be enough. You saw what we were up against the other day, and that was only a small portion of just one company of guards. To fight an army, you need an army. It's as simple as that."

As simple as that? Hardly!

Katerina lifted her eyebrows as Dylan sank suddenly lower in his seat. "Simple? I get what you're saying, Cass, and while I'd love to have an army to fight alongside it's not like that's the easiest thing to come by. To have an army, you need to have a kingdom first. And it's not like, as the leader of the rebel forces, I'm going to be on good speaking terms with any of the other royals."

She thought her point was rather obvious, but she seemed to have said the magic words. The second they were past her lips Cassiel turned to Dylan with a look of scarcely contained triumph.

"That's right, Katerina. To have an army, you need to have a kingdom first. You need to have the support of a member of a royal family."

Time seemed to slow down as he leaned across the table, staring at his best friend.

"How about it, Hale? You know any places like that?"

"YOU DON'T HAVE TO DO this," Katerina said for what felt like the millionth time. "I'm telling you—you don't have to do this."

Dylan never slowed his pace. If anything, he moved even faster through the trees. "Yes, I do."

They had been walking since early that morning, heading in a straight line due North. At first, Katerina hadn't understood why he'd been so uncomfortable when they'd first touched down. The way his eyes drifted with sickening familiarity over everything they happened to see. She didn't make the connection that Belaria was the northernmost kingdom when she'd picked a random direction in which to fly. She didn't make the connection until Cassiel said the name *Hale* the previous night.

"I know you think you do," she said quickly, hurrying after him, "but you should know that I'm not asking. I understand perfectly well why you left, Dylan, and there are other ways of getting the help we need. No one here is forcing you to go back—"

He stopped so abruptly that she ran straight into him, rubbing her nose and squinting up at him in the bright morning sun.

"Last night, I watched you sacrifice everything you had for this cause. Show the entire world your secret, lay everything you are on the line." His eyes glowed with unspeakable pride before cooling as they glanced towards the city. "What would it say about me if I didn't do the same?"

It was hard to argue with that kind of logic. It was hard to argue at all when he made her point for her. When he was doing exactly the thing she happened to secretly want.

Yes—I want him to be a prince. I want him to take back his throne. To accept his birthright. Just like me.

The reasons for this were too numerous to count. Most of them revolved directly around the fact that she believed he was robbing himself of a future he so obviously deserved by putting on a ranger's cloak and refusing to be called by his rightful name. But there were other reasons as well. Reasons so new and unknown she was having trouble solidifying them herself.

But somewhere deep in the back of her mind, she knew that she would one day have to end up with a prince. Someone of royal blood. Someone in a position similar to her own.

That someone could never be Dylan Aires.

But maybe, just maybe, it could be Dylan Hale.

"As long as you're sure." She scurried after him as he surged forward once more, striding deliberately through the trees. "As long as you're *absolutely* sure. Because I don't want to be the one forcing your hand here. And, as self-righteous as he is, it's not Cassiel's place either. This is a decision you should make in your own time. One that should have nothing to do with—"

He kissed her. Sweeping her off her feet.

"—me."

She stared up at him breathlessly when he pulled away, his eyes twinkling down at her with that ever- familiar smile. It was a look she knew she'd remember for the rest of her life. The look he always gave her right before their lives were about to change.

"You talk a lot when you get nervous. Have I ever told you that?"

And, so, it was decided.

Just a few sleepless hours after causing the greatest uproar the five kingdoms had ever seen, the six friends were venturing once more into uncharted territory. Leaving behind the land of the rebels to actively seek out a royal house. Only, for one of their members, it was simply going home.

Dylan stopped abruptly when they came to the city gates. Wide pillars of solid ivory that wound about in delicate patterns, twisting up into a pointed arch. It was beautiful but intimidating at the same time. A bit like its renegade prince.

"Are you okay?" Katerina asked softly, placing her hand on his arm.

He nodded, gazing up at the pillars with a truly indescribable look in his eyes. "It's just... I honestly never thought I'd come back."

She squeezed his hand as Cassiel came to stand beside them. They waited a moment, and then together the three of them pushed open the gate and took their first steps inside...

Chapter 15

The capital city of Belaria was exactly as Katerina had always imagined it.

Pristine. Decadent. A stunning display of old-world architecture mixed with the natural greenery of open space. White walls, stained-glass windows, cobblestone streets. A haven for merchants and artisans, musicians and politicians, sculptors and poets. All living in the same intricate labyrinth of buildings, all twisting around the same crystalline river.

A river that led straight to the royal palace.

Dylan's eyes flickered up to the white towers, and for the second time it seemed like he couldn't catch his breath. "Just...just give me a second."

Katerina and Cassiel exchanged a quick look. The ranger they knew never needed to 'take a second.' But perhaps the prince did.

"Sweetie?" She walked over to him, placing a cautious hand on his back. "We can do this in stages, you know. You coming here was a big step—we don't have to go to the palace right away."

Cassiel nodded sympathetically, gesturing to a nearby inn. "Why don't we get a room for the night? Find a tavern, get you a drink—"

"No," Dylan said abruptly, a look of sudden determination sharpening his eyes. "This is supposed to be my big homecoming, right? Might as well get the celebrations underway."

Without a moment's pause he walked right up to a royal guard stationed in the center of the town square, tasked with keeping the peace.

He flashed the man a tight smile before lifting his head with all the authority he could muster.

"I require an escort to the palace at once. My name is Dylan Hale, only son of Aldrich Hale, King of the Northern Kingdom. If it's all the same to you, I've come to take back my crown."

Only Dylan would be so bold. Only Dylan would make such an entrance. And only Dylan could look so surprised when it all blew up in his face.

"Dylan Hale?" the guard repeated, slow and deliberate.

Dylan nodded, then froze in shock as five more guards appeared out of nowhere, gripping him firmly by the arms, their weapons jangling noisily by their sides.

"We've been expecting you."

The man clapped a silver chain around his wrist.

"You're under arrest."

THE END

Forever Blurb

She will fight for what is hers.
What can you do when the people you trust, are the ones you should fear the most?

After months of staring down death and escaping danger at every turn, Katerina and her friends find themselves in the last place they'd ever expect. A dungeon. And not the prince's dungeon either. This betrayal struck a little closer to home.

With time running out and Kailas' coronation looming on the horizon, the six friends must find a way to make peace with the past to have any chance at a future. Old alliances must be rekindled. Old grudges must be put away. But there are some scars that never fully heal.

Keep your friends close, and your enemies closer. But *this* enemy, turned out to be closer than Katerina ever thought...

...can she ever take back the throne?

The Queen's Alpha Series

Eternal
Everlasting
Unceasing
Evermore
Forever

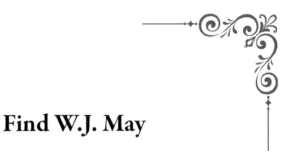

Find W.J. May

Website:
http://www.wanitamay.yolasite.com
Facebook:
https://www.facebook.com/pages/Author-WJ-May-FAN-PAGE/
141170442608149
Newsletter:
SIGN UP FOR W.J. May's Newsletter to find out about new releases,
updates, cover reveals and even freebies!
http://eepurl.com/97aYf

More books by W.J. May

The Chronicles of Kerrigan

Book I - *Rae of Hope* is FREE!
　　Book Trailer:
http://www.youtube.com/watch?v=gILAwXxx8MU
Book II - *Dark Nebula*
Book Trailer:
http://www.youtube.com/watch?v=Ca24STi_bFM
Book III - *House of Cards*
Book IV - *Royal Tea*
Book V - *Under Fire*
Book VI - *End in Sight*
Book VII – *Hidden Darkness*
Book VIII – *Twisted Together*
Book IX – *Mark of Fate*
Book X – *Strength & Power*
Book XI – *Last One Standing*
BOOK XII – *Rae of Light*

PREQUEL –
Christmas Before the Magic
Question the Darkness
Into the Darkness
Fight the Darkness
Alone the Darkness
Lost the Darkness

SEQUEL –
Matter of Time
Time Piece
Second Chance

Glitch in Time
Our Time
Precious Time

Hidden Secrets Saga:
Download Seventh Mark part 1 & 2 For FREE
Book Trailer:
http://www.youtube.com/watch?v=Y-_vVYC1gvo

Like most teenagers, Rouge is trying to figure out who she is and what she wants to be. With little knowledge about her past, she has questions but has never tried to find the answers. Everything changes when she befriends a strangely intoxicating family. Siblings Grace and Michael, appear to have secrets which seem connected to Rouge. Her hunch is confirmed when a horrible incident occurs at an outdoor party. Rouge may be the only one who can find the answer.

An ancient journal, a Sioghra necklace and a special mark force life-altering decisions for a girl who grew up unprepared to fight for her life or others.

All secrets have a cost and Rouge's determination to find the truth can only lead to trouble...or something even more sinister.

RADIUM HALOS - THE SENSELESS SERIES
Book 1 is FREE:

Everyone needs to be a hero at one point in their life.

The small town of Elliot Lake will never be the same again.

Caught in a sudden thunderstorm, Zoe, a high school senior from Elliot Lake, and five of her friends take shelter in an abandoned uranium mine. Over the next few days, Zoe's hearing sharpens drastically, beyond what any normal human being can detect. She tells her friends, only to learn that four others have an increased sense as well. Only Kieran, the new boy from Scotland, isn't affected.

Fashioning themselves into superheroes, the group tries to stop the strange occurrences happening in their little town. Muggings, break-ins, disappearances, and murder begin to hit too close to home. It leads the team to think someone knows about their secret - someone who wants them all dead.

An incredulous group of heroes. A traitor in the midst. Some dreams are written in blood.

Courage Runs Red
The Blood Red Series
Book 1 is FREE

WHAT IF COURAGE WAS your only option?

When Kallie lands a college interview with the city's new hot-shot police officer, she has no idea everything in her life is about to change. The detective is young, handsome and seems to have an unnatural ability to stop the increasing local crime rate. Detective Liam's particular interest in Kallie sends her heart and head stumbling over each other.

When a raging blood feud between vampires spills into her home, Kallie gets caught in the middle. Torn between love and family loyalty she must find the courage to fight what she fears the most and possibly risk everything, even if it means dying for those she loves.

Daughter of Darkness
VICTORIA
Only Death Could Stop Her Now
The Daughters of Darkness is a series of female heroines who may or may not know each other, but all have the same father, Vlad Montour. Victoria is a Hunter Vampire

Don't miss out!

Click the button below and you can sign up to receive emails whenever W.J. May publishes a new book. There's no charge and no obligation.

https://books2read.com/r/B-A-SSF-BZQR

Connecting independent readers to independent writers.

Did you love *Evermore*? Then you should read *The Chronicles of Kerrigan Box Set Books # 1 - 6* by W.J. May!

Join Rae Kerrigan & start an amazing adventure! By USA Today Bestseller WJ May

The Chronicles of Kerrigan BoxSet

Bk 1 - Rae of Hope

How hard do you have to shake the family tree to find the truth about the past?

15 yr-old Rae Kerrigan never knew her family's history. Her mother & father died when she was young and it's only when she accepts a scholarship to the prestigious Guilder Boarding School in England that a mysterious family secret is revealed.

Will the sins of the father be the sins of the daughter?

As Rae struggles with new friends, a new school & a star-struck forbidden love, she must also face the ultimate challenge: receive a tattoo on her 16th birthday with specific powers that may bind her to an unspeakable darkness. It's up to Rae to undo the darkness in her family's past and have a ray of hope for her future.

Bk 2 - Dark Nebula

Nothing is as it seems anymore.

Leery from the horrifying incident at the end of her first year at Guilder, Rae's determined to learn more about her new tattoo. Her expectations are high, but all hopes of happiness turn into shattered dreams the moment she steps back on campus.

Lies & secrets are everywhere, and a betrayal cuts Rae deeply. Among her conflicts & enemies, it appears her father is reaching out from beyond the grave to ruin her life. With no one to trust, Rae doesn't know who to turn to for help.

Has her destiny been written? Or will she become the one thing she hates the most-her father's prodigy.

Bk 3 - House of Cards

Rae Kerrigan is 3months away from graduating from Guilder. She's now moonlighting as an operative for the Privy Council, a black ops division for British Intelligence. She's given a mentor, Jennifer, who fights like a demon.Rae finds a strange maternal bond with her. At the same time, she finds a new friend when Devon disappoints her once again.

When the Privy Council ask for her help, she finds a friend, and a link, to the Xavier Knights—another agency similar to the PCs.

Will she lose herself in the confusions of the past and present? What will it mean for her future?

Book 4 - Royal Tea

The Queen of England has requested the help of the Privy Council. Someone is trying to kill her son's fiancé. The HRH Prince plans to marry a commoner, and his bride has a secret no one knows but the Privy Council. She has a tatù. When the Privy Council turns to Rae for help, she can't possibly say no; not even when they make Devon her partner for this assignment.

Rae would rather be anywhere but with Devon, especially since she believes her mother to be alive, despite the Privy Council's assurances to the contrary. How can Rae find proof of life for her mother, come to terms with her feelings for Devon, and manage to save the Princess, all while dressed for tea?

When the enigma, the secrets and the skeletons in the closet begin to be exposed, can Rae handle the truth?

Book 5 - Under Fire

Rae Kerrigan is determined to find her mother. No amount of convincing from Devon, or the Privy Council, is going to make her believe her mother is not alive, and Rae will stop at nothing to find her.

Torn between friendship and loyalty, Rae must also choose between Luke and Devon. She can't continue to deny, or fool herself, any longer. The heart wants what the heart wants.

Book 6 - End in Sight

When life couldn't get anymore confusing, fate steps in and throws a curveball.

Also by W.J. May

Bit-Lit Series
Lost Vampire
Cost of Blood
Price of Death

Blood Red Series
Courage Runs Red
The Night Watch
Marked by Courage
Forever Night

Daughters of Darkness: Victoria's Journey
Victoria
Huntress
Coveted (A Vampire & Paranormal Romance)
Twisted

Hidden Secrets Saga

Strength & Power
Last One Standing
Rae of Light
The Chronicles of Kerrigan Box Set Books # 1 - 6

The Chronicles of Kerrigan: Gabriel
Living in the Past
Staring at the Future
Present For Today

The Chronicles of Kerrigan Prequel
Question the Darkness
Into the Darkness
Fight the Darkness
Alone in the Darkness
Lost in Darkness
Christmas Before the Magic
The Chronicles of Kerrigan Prequel Series Books #1-3

The Chronicles of Kerrigan Sequel
A Matter of Time
Time Piece
Second Chance
Glitch in Time
Our Time
Precious Time

The Hidden Secrets Saga
Seventh Mark (part 1 & 2)

The Queen's Alpha Series
Eternal
Everlasting
Unceasing
Evermore
Forever

The Senseless Series
Radium Halos
Radium Halos - Part 2
Nonsense

Standalone
Shadow of Doubt (Part 1 & 2)
Five Shades of Fantasy
Shadow of Doubt - Part 1
Shadow of Doubt - Part 2
Four and a Half Shades of Fantasy
Dream Fighter
What Creeps in the Night
Forest of the Forbidden
Arcane Forest: A Fantasy Anthology

Made in the USA
Monee, IL
11 January 2021